THE
LIGHTHOUSE

STRIPES PUBLISHING LIMITED
An imprint of the Little Tiger Group
1 Coda Studios, 189 Munster Road,
London SW6 6AW

www.littletiger.co.uk

Imported into the EEA by Penguin Random House Ireland,
Morrison Chambers, 32 Nassu Street, Dublin D02 YH68

First published in Great Britain in 2022
Text copyright © Alex Bell, 2022
Cover illustration copyright © Stripes Publishing Limited, 2022

ISBN: 978-1-78895-151-7

Printed and bound in the UK.

The Forest Stewardship Council® (FSC®) is a global, not-for-profit organization dedicated to the
promotion of responsible forest management worldwide. FSC defines standards based on agreed
principles for responsible forest stewardship that are supported by environmental, social, and economic
stakeholders. To learn more, visit www.fsc.org

10 9 8 7 6 5 4 3 2 1

THE LIGHTHOUSE

ALEX BELL

RED
EYE

Prologue

It was Kenzie's idea to play Truth or Dare that night. It wasn't as if there was much else to do on Bird Rock. No cinemas, no cafés, not even any phone reception. The island was just a lump of jagged black rock in the middle of the cold, pitiless sea. Nothing but birds, a few stone bothies and the lighthouse.

Don't go near the lighthouse…

The three teenagers had all been given the same instruction by their parents when they had come to Bird Rock for the gannet hunt. It wasn't a question of superstition, the adults insisted, only a question of sense. The lighthouse had been uninhabited for years and might not be safe.

"I'll go first," Kenzie said, tossing another log on their campfire and sending up a shower of red sparks that made the shadows leap and dance around them.

"All right," her friend Emily replied. "Truth or Dare?"

Kenzie smiled. "Dare. And make it a good one this time."

"I've got an idea," Will said, rubbing his hands together. He was Kenzie's brother, and they looked very alike with their fair hair and grey eyes. "I dare you to go into the lighthouse."

All three of them glanced at the old building. It stood tall and straight, like a finger pointing directly up into the night sky, its bright light flashing out a warning at regular intervals. The word *lighthouse* seemed to hang in the air, and it felt inevitable that someone had suggested it. After all, wasn't that why Kenzie had wanted to play Truth or Dare in the first place? Wasn't that why they'd chosen to build their campfire right here, practically in the building's shadow? They could hear the invisible sea sucking hungrily at the cliffs below. The lighthouse towering over them felt like one of those 'bad-influence' friends – the kind that would lead you astray. The kind that wasn't really a friend at all.

Will knew that his sister liked a challenge, that she

wanted someone to dare her to go inside the disused building. "It's haunted, you know," he said, grinning.

"I don't think we should joke about it," Emily said, looking uncomfortable. "My uncle saw something in there years ago."

The other two went quiet. Emily very rarely talked about her uncle. He was renowned in their village for the wrong reasons, always doing or saying strange things. Normally Emily seemed embarrassed to be associated with him and would try to pretend he didn't exist. It was rare for her to mention him at all.

"I didn't know your uncle ever came to Bird Rock," Kenzie finally said.

"Just once," Emily replied. "With the gannet hunters when he was our age. He refused to come back after that."

"Well, what did he see then?" Will asked.

"He went into the lighthouse with his friends," Emily said. "And he said he saw white hands pressing against the windows from the outside. But when the other hunters went to look, there was no one there."

Their eyes flicked towards the dilapidated building once again. It was too dark to see in any detail, but they knew that the paint was peeling from its exterior, and the door was practically falling off its hinges. The windows were dark and the rooms empty. There was no one there. There hadn't been for years.

"That's not all," Emily said. "My uncle said there are words you mustn't ever say inside the lighthouse."

Will looked delighted by this. "Go on," he encouraged. "What were they?"

"*I know you're there.*" Emily whispered the phrase, as if concerned that the lighthouse might hear her from a distance.

"What happens if you do?" Kenzie asked, looking more curious than frightened.

"He wouldn't tell me," Emily replied. "But it's something bad. Especially if you say it three times. He only managed to say the words twice and … something bad happened, but he'd never tell us what."

"Well, this just makes it an even better dare!" Will exclaimed. "How about it, Kenz? Is a haunted lighthouse too much for you?"

His sister snorted. "As if! I'm not scared of that old place. In fact, I'd happily live in it while we're on the island. It's got to be more comfortable than those damp bothies."

"Please don't," Emily said.

"Come on, Em—"

"No, *really*!" Emily said with unusual sharpness in her voice. "I don't think we should. Whether you believe in ghosts or not, people have died there. It's … it's disrespectful."

Kenzie placed a hand on her friend's arm. "It's only a bit of fun," she said. "But if it upsets you that much then we can do something else—"

Will immediately started making chicken noises. "You're just looking for an excuse not to do it!" he said, pointing at his sister triumphantly. "You're scared!"

Kenzie bristled. "I am not! Don't be a knob!"

"There's only one way to prove it," Will replied. He offered Emily a smile. "There's literally nothing else to do here, and it's not like you have to walk into the lighthouse yourself. Kenzie will go alone. That's the point of the dare. I haven't even asked her to say those cursed words of yours – she just has to poke her head inside. What could be wrong with that?"

"We'll do this one dare to shut Will up, and then we'll go back to camp and toast some marshmallows, OK?" Kenzie said, giving her friend's arm a squeeze.

Emily tried to protest further, but it was no use. Kenzie knew that Will would forever taunt her for chickening out if she didn't go through with it now, and there was no way she was going to put up with that.

"I'll go in, count to five and then come straight back out," she said to Emily. "You won't know I'm gone."

"No cheating," Will warned. "And no lingering in the doorway. You have to actually stand inside."

"No problem," Kenzie replied, rolling her eyes.

She turned to go, using her phone to illuminate her way over the loose rocks and gravel. She reached the lighthouse's front door a few moments later, and the other two saw it open at her touch. Pausing on the threshold, she glanced back once, raised her hand in a wave and then disappeared inside.

"One…" Emily muttered under her breath, "two, three, four, five."

She and Will both looked at the door, expecting Kenzie to emerge at any moment, her blond ponytail swinging as she bounded over to them triumphantly. But there was no sign of her. As the minutes stretched on, the lighthouse doorway remained a dark, empty rectangle.

"I don't like this," Emily said. "Something isn't right."

"She's probably just having a look around," Will replied.

"Why would she do that?" Emily asked. "She said she'd be right back. She promised."

"Well, maybe she's just messing with us then," Will said. "Hiding to see if we'll go in after her."

"I'm not going in there!" Emily said at once.

"You won't have to, Em," Will replied. "She'll get bored and come out eventually. You'll see."

But time continued to pass, and soon Kenzie had been gone almost twenty minutes. Emily was so fidgety by this point that she could barely keep still.

"Will, I'm *really* starting to get worried now," she said.

She hoped he would be concerned too, but to her dismay he only laughed.

"Let's just go back to camp," he said, standing up and stretching his back. "She'll be right behind us when she realizes we're not going after her."

"But we can't just *leave* her in there!" Emily said, scrambling to her feet too. "She might be—"

She broke off just then because suddenly a light came on inside the lighthouse – a window near the top of the tower was filled with a sickly yellow glow.

Emily let out a cry of alarm, and Will frowned. "What the hell is she doing up there? She'll break her neck on that rickety staircase. I suppose I'll just have to go and fetch her after all." He glanced at Emily. "Wait here if you want."

"By *myself*?"

"Well, it's either that or come with me. Up to you."

"Fine, I'll come," Emily said, swallowing her dread.

Will was already leaving, his boots crunching loudly over the gravel. The lighthouse grew taller and taller the closer they got. Emily was certain the door had been open just a moment ago, but now it was closed again. Will pushed, and it swung forward with a loud creaking of hinges that made Emily jump.

"Kenzie!" he shouted. "Very funny, now let's go! You're freaking Emily out."

There was no response, so Will went inside, and Emily reluctantly followed. A gust of wind blew through, and the door slammed closed behind them, swallowing them up. All was quiet outside.

Exactly fourteen and a half minutes later, the

door burst open again, and Emily stumbled outside, gasping for breath, barely managing to remain upright. She couldn't stay in that lighthouse another minute, or even another second, not for anyone. She didn't look back, or speak, or pause. She didn't try to break the deafening silence in any way. She just ran as fast as she could, desperate to put as much space as possible between herself and the lighthouse of Bird Rock.

An Account of Bird Rock by Jess Oliver, Aged Fifteen

It's hard to talk about Bird Rock without sounding like I've totally lost it. And it's especially hard to talk about Bird Rock in a way that's honest and tells the complete story. I wish we'd never gone to that awful place. But I've got to write it down because something terrible happened there. Something that needs to be undone.

We left someone behind. Even now, I can hardly believe that we did it, but Bird Rock messes up your head. It confuses you as to what's real and what isn't. It's hard to explain to someone who's never been there, but my story might help you understand, just a little. So here goes.

My name is Jess Oliver, and this is a true story... Or at least as truthful as I can make it.

Chapter One

The Day Before the Island

My dad's work as an ornithologist took him all over the world, and ever since he and Mum divorced eight years ago, we hardly ever saw him except in the summer holidays. For two weeks a year, he would leave his new family behind in Scotland and deign to spend a fortnight with Rosie and me. He usually booked a hotel in London, and we spent the days traipsing around the city like tourists, visiting museums and doing different escape rooms.

Personally, I'd rather have been hanging out with my friends, but Rosie looked forward to the holiday with Dad all year. Perhaps the difference was that I was fifteen and Rosie was only twelve. I'd enjoyed Dad's visits too when I was her age, but they felt weird and a bit flat to me now, like we were all pretending to be something we weren't.

"Your father has a big project on the island," Mum had told me. "Bird Rock is only habitable during the summer apparently, so the trip can't be delayed and … well, it'll be an adventure, won't it? Staying in an actual lighthouse. I'm sure the island is very beautiful at this time of year. There's all that wildlife, the rugged coasts and ocean sunsets. We thought it would be the perfect opportunity for Rosie to enjoy her photography and for you to do some stargazing away from all the light pollution."

I hated it when my mum did this – made out that something was being arranged for *our* benefit when we both knew it was actually all about what was most convenient for Dad, but it seemed we had no choice in the matter. We were being shipped off to the Outer Hebrides for two weeks whether we liked it or not.

And as the day got closer, I dreaded leaving more and more. My friends all seemed to have tons of exciting plans arranged – shopping trips and music festivals, sleepovers and movie nights, glamping and sunbathing. All stuff that I would have to miss out on.

To make it even worse, Dad's new family would be

there this time. His wife Kate was an ornithologist too, and they had a six-year-old son, our half-brother Charlie. I'd only met him once before, a couple of years ago at an awkward Rainforest Café lunch. He'd cried because they'd run out of mozzarella sticks and then spilled his drink everywhere. It had been both embarrassing and annoying.

When I'd googled the island, I'd found that Mum had been playing it down a bit when she described it as 'small'. In fact, it was one of the most remote islands in the entire UK. We'd literally be the only people there. There weren't even any shops or cafés. The only buildings were stone bothies that had been built by monks hundreds of years ago. And, of course, the lighthouse itself. Rosie was very excited about the lighthouse.

The morning we were due to leave, she came bounding into my bedroom where I was trying to panic-pack and threw herself down on my bed.

"Guess what?" she asked.

"Would it kill you to knock?" I sighed.

Boundaries and personal space seemed to be

concepts that Rosie really didn't understand, despite my best attempts to explain them to her.

"The lighthouse we're staying in is *haunted*!" She beamed, as if she'd just told me we were staying in a hotel, and that it had *five* stars.

Although there were three years between us, people often said that Rosie and I looked a lot alike, with our green eyes and honey-coloured hair, but the similarities ended there. Personality-wise, we couldn't have been more different. I liked science; Rosie liked spooks. I liked telescopes; Rosie liked tarot cards. I liked shopping with my friends; Rosie liked holding seances with hers. Mum thought it was odd that Rosie was into all that spooky stuff given that she'd been so ill as a young kid, but I reckoned it was probably a big part of why she'd become interested in the first place.

Today my little sister was wearing a black T-shirt with a cartoon ghost printed on it, along with the words: *I Believe.* And as usual she wore a selection of crystal jewellery – her favourite rose-quartz angel hung on a chain around her neck, and she also had on a lace-agate bracelet. Thanks to Rosie, I knew a lot more about crystals and their meanings than

I ever really wanted to. Rose quartz represented unconditional love, and the angel pendant had been my gift to her last Christmas. The pale blue lace agate was supposed to encourage self-confidence.

"The first two lighthouse keepers ever to stay there went missing, and no one knows what happened to them!" my sister went on gleefully. "Here, look at this!"

She thrust her phone at me. She'd been going on about a reported sighting of Bigfoot last week, and it had been UFOs spotted flying over Sainsbury's the week before that. This time it was lighthouses. The lighthouse on Bird Rock in particular. The article read:

Finn Lewis and Niall Abernathy were both experienced keepers of many years. They'd been stationed at the new lighthouse on Bird Rock for only a month in 1807 when the unthinkable happened. Cut off from the outside world, no one had any inkling that anything was wrong until a couple of passing ships reported that the lantern wasn't operating in bad weather.

The Northern Lighthouse Board attempted to communicate with the men via radio, but their calls went unanswered. Finally a relief team was sent to investigate. When they entered the lighthouse, they knew at once that something was terribly wrong. There was no sign of either Finn Lewis or Niall Abernathy. The men had simply vanished, yet their boots were lined up on the shoe rack, and their waterproof coats still hung from pegs.

Not only that but a long-cold supper lay untouched upon the table – a feast for the flies. There was no sign of any disturbance – it was as if the men had simply got up one day and walked out. There was no way they could have left the island without a boat, and yet there was no trace of them.

The Northern Lighthouse Board officially concluded that the two men must have been swept out to sea by a storm. But why would keepers of their experience head outside during such inclement weather in the first place? And without their boots and waterproof coats? And why were the final pages of their logbooks filled with such peculiar reports?

Both men had made entries detailing how the other had been behaving strangely. In addition, Abernathy reported hearing odd sounds coming from within the lighthouse itself – tapping, and knocking, and scratching at the walls…

The mystery persists to this day. Although no further keepers have vanished from the island, the lighthouse at Bird Rock certainly seems a fated and unfortunate place. Many *of the subsequent keepers asked for transfers or were removed to asylums, unable to cope with the isolation, the fog and the thousands of birds.*

We will never know what truly happened to those first keepers over two hundred years ago, but some say they're still there. That they never left and are still committed to doing their duty, even in death, manning the light to warn passing ships away from whatever danger lies at the heart of Bird Rock.

"I'm going to be rich!" Rosie exclaimed gleefully, as I handed the phone back. "I just need *one* photo of a ghost in the lighthouse, and I'm bound to win that competition!"

It took me a moment to realize what she was talking about, but then I remembered the photography competition she'd been fixated on for days. It had been set up by the Society for Paranormal Research, or something like that – one of those weird groups she followed – and invited participants to submit haunted photos. Apparently, the winner would be awarded a £1,000 cash prize.

"It'll be pretty tricky capturing a ghost on film," I said, turning back to my packing. "Seeing as there's no such thing. You'll have to create another one of your fakes."

Rosie had become pretty good at trick photography recently and knew how to make all kinds of special effects with her cameras.

"Well, you can look at the stars while I look for ghosts," Rosie said. "And then we'll both be happy."

"Awesome," I replied. "Now would you mind getting out of the way? I'm trying to finish packing."

"You should have done it last night like Mum told you to," Rosie said, poking her tongue out at me and then scooting from the room before I could whack her with a pillow.

No thanks to Rosie, I just about managed to finish before the taxi came to take us to the airport. The flight to the Outer Hebrides took three hours, including a quick stopover at Glasgow, and when we stepped out of the airport at the other end I couldn't believe how much colder it was. It had been a sunny twenty-five degrees back in London, but here it was barely fifteen, and the sky was choked with thick grey clouds.

I flagged down a taxi and asked the driver to take us to the town. We were staying the night in a youth hostel before catching a boat the next morning. Rosie and I spent a very boring hour walking round the quiet little town and then headed back to the hostel for the rest of the afternoon. We had dinner in the canteen and hung out in the lounge for a while, playing table football. After a while, Rosie called it a night and went upstairs. I promised I'd be right behind her, but first I wandered into the small library, intending to take a look at the lighthouse photos I'd spotted from the doorway earlier.

Only there was someone already there, standing before the photos with his back to me – a tall blond man. He made a sound, which I thought was a snort of laughter at first, but then realized it was a sob. His shoulders were actually shaking. I froze, wondering whether I should ask if he needed any help, or if that would just be weird...

Before I could decide, a boy about my age walked in from the side entrance. I couldn't help noticing that he was very good-looking, with fair, windswept hair and grey eyes. He didn't see me – his gaze went straight to the man, and he hurried over. I guessed at once they must be father and son because they looked so alike.

"Dad," he said softly, reaching out a hand. "Can I—"

I was shocked when the older man practically smacked the boy's hand away. "You've done enough," he snarled.

Now that the older man had turned, I could see the tears on his cheeks and that his eyes were bloodshot.

"Let's get one thing straight," he said, his voice shaking slightly. "I'm only here because your mother begged me to come with you. It's breaking her heart that you're set on this, so I'm here for her sake, not yours. If you cared about her at all, you'd be at home right now." A pleading tone came into his voice. "We could leave tonight and be back in time for breakfast. It's not too late."

A carefully blank look came over the boy's face, and suddenly there was a coolness in his grey eyes, but his voice was calm as he slowly shook his head. "It is too late."

The beseeching expression on his father's face vanished, twisting into something that was more like hatred. "Too bloody selfish," he spat. "Is there no end to what you'll put us through?"

His voice broke on the final words, and another sob burst from his chest. Then, to my dismay, he strode straight towards the doorway. It was too late to avoid being seen so I just stepped to one side to let him pass. Then he was gone, and I found myself making awkward eye contact with the boy. I was mortified to have been discovered standing there, as if I'd been eavesdropping, and I felt my mouth twitch – something that happened whenever I was massively uncomfortable.

Unfortunately, the boy noticed, misinterpreted it and said in a dangerously quiet voice, "Don't even think about laughing at him."

"Oh! I wasn't!" I began. "I mean, I wouldn't! I was just—"

But the boy was already walking past me. "I really don't care," he said. There was no anger in his tone, only a sort of heavy tiredness.

As he left, I cursed myself for being such an idiot and lingering like that, but it was too late to undo it now. And it wasn't as if I'd see the boy or his father again anyway. I took a deep breath and then walked over to the lighthouse photos on the walls.

Could they have had anything to do with what had upset the man?

The photos were taken at different times and seasons by the looks of it. When I peered at them more closely, I saw that they all had the same smudge in one of the windows up near the top of the tower – a smudge that looked kind of person-shaped, like there was someone there, staring out to sea. I shivered suddenly and rubbed my arms.

Mum seemed to think it was amazing that we were staying in a lighthouse, but it sounded a bit depressing to me, and all I really wanted was to be back home with my friends. Rosie would have a nice time, though, and if my sister was happy then I was happy too. After all, at least I wasn't visiting her in hospital like I had been during previous summers. We were spending the holidays together, doing something normal, and it was bound to be beautiful on Bird Rock, as Mum had said. So perhaps it would be OK. Perhaps it might even be fun. Perhaps it would be the best summer ever.

Chapter Two

Day One on the Island

Rosie and I were up so early the next morning that there was no one else in the canteen when we had our breakfast. We wolfed down some dry croissants, then went down to the harbour and waited for the boat that Dad had said would take us the rest of the way to Bird Rock. There were no scheduled ferries or sightseeing tours to the island. Absolutely nobody went there, which wasn't surprising given there was nothing to see but birds. And apparently, if the weather was bad, you couldn't land there at all. I wondered if this would be the case today because the grey waves were churning restlessly. Apart from a couple of stray fishermen working on their boats, there was no one else around. Time dragged on, and finally a wiry, middle-aged man appeared in front of us.

"You the Oliver girls?" he asked. "Jess and Rosie?"

"Yes, that's us."

"I'm Jim. I've come to take you to Bird Rock."

"Oh. Are we actually going today then?" I asked. "I thought the sea looked too rough."

A strange little smile twisted one corner of his mouth, like a grimace. "That?" He jerked his thumb at the sea. "That's nothing. About the best it gets around here, in fact. I'd use the bathroom at the café over there if you haven't already."

"Isn't there one on the boat?" I asked.

He smiled again. "Aye, but we're sailing on that." He pointed along the pier to a tiny tin bucket of a vessel. "You'll probably want to go below decks as little as possible. Not the best smell down there, if you get my drift. And four hours on the water is a long time."

I stared at him. "I'm sorry, what? Four *hours*?"

He raised an eyebrow. "You didn't know?"

"No! No one said anything about a four-hour boat trip!"

I'd assumed it would be half an hour or so. Rosie looked equally horrified. Jim just seemed amused, which only made me feel more irritated.

"If you try to find Bird Rock on a map, you'd be looking for a speck way out in the North Atlantic, about the size of a biscuit crumb," he said cheerfully. "In fact, it's so small, it's not even marked on a lot of charts. One of the remotest islands in the Outer Hebrides is Bird Rock. Heck of a place to get to."

I felt suddenly furious with Dad. He must have withheld this information from us on purpose.

Rosie and I both used the café toilets as Jim had suggested, then collected our bags and headed towards the small boat. The sight of it reminded me that once we were at Bird Rock we wouldn't be able to leave again until it came to collect us in two weeks. We'd be stuck there, like prisoners.

"Sit down and hold on," Jim instructed.

We squeezed into the narrow plastic seats inside the wheelhouse, then Jim revved the throttle and we pulled out of the harbour towards the open sea. I'd never been on such a small boat before, and it lurched, rolled and moved much more than I'd been expecting. I had to brace with my feet to stay stable in my chair.

The journey was horrible. Before long, we'd lost

sight of the mainland and were surrounded by the grey water of the North Atlantic stretching out in all directions. Since the sky was grey too, it was hard to tell where the sea ended and the sky began. My skin felt dried out and sticky with salt. The wind rushed straight through the wheelhouse, along with frequent bursts of icy spray.

"This island better be an absolute paradise," I said to Rosie, raising my voice to be heard over the din.

She nodded, looking miserable and more than a little green. I was so cross with Dad – I just couldn't believe that we were stuck on this boat for *four hours* with nothing to do. I didn't even dare take my phone out of my pocket to make the most of the last remaining bars of reception, in case it went flying over the side.

Rosie looked more and more ill as time went on. I gave her a nudge and mouthed, *You OK?*

She shook her head, then a few minutes later, lurched over to the side of the boat and vomited. I felt pretty queasy myself and was definitely regretting the breakfast I'd eaten at the hostel. Luckily my seasickness was mild and I was never actually sick on the boat, but Rosie threw up over and over again.

As usual, the sight of her being in any way unwell tied my stomach up into tight little knots of anxiety. I knew this was nothing like before – she was just being seasick. But still. It reminded me of that bad, dark time, which made an invisible weight settle on my shoulders. Finally Rosie slumped down next to me, exhausted. I longed to reach out to her, to ask if she was all right and whether there was anything I could do, but I didn't dare do more than briefly squeeze her shoulder. Rosie couldn't stand people fussing and fretting over her. I guessed it reminded her of the bad time too.

"Gets a lot of people like that," Jim said, giving Rosie a sympathetic look.

I checked my watch after a while, hoping we might be more than halfway there, but to my dismay barely an hour had passed. The thought of this going on for another three was hell.

"I'm going to murder Dad," I said to Rosie, who nodded bleakly.

We seemed to pass into a sort of strange bubble where time no longer existed at all, and it began to feel as if we'd never get to the island. Until I started to become aware of the most awful, fetid stench.

At first it was just a waft invading my nose for a moment or two before being swallowed up by the sea breeze. But soon enough it hung heavy and ripe in the air around us, so disgusting and strong that I thought the spray must have deposited a load of dead, rotting fish on the deck somewhere.

"What's that gross smell?" I finally asked.

Jim glanced at me, and his mouth twisted into a half-smile. "That's Bird Rock," he said.

Rosie and I frowned at each other. The island wasn't even in sight yet, so what could he possibly mean by that? But the next moment I realized that it *had* appeared — it was just difficult to spot against the cloudy sky. I'd read that the island was made of jagged black rock, yet the one before us was white. Surely Jim wasn't taking us to the wrong place?

When I asked about it, he shook his head. "The island isn't white. Just looks that way because of all the gannets. There's thousands of 'em. Around one hundred and fifty thousand, to be exact. Their guano creates that smell."

"What's guano?" Rosie asked.

"Bird poo," Jim replied. "Island's covered in it." He gave that half-smile again — a smile that didn't reach his eyes. "Delightful, isn't it?"

We could only stare at him in horror. When Mum had spoken of a bird island, I'd imagined something pretty and lovely, but if the smell was this bad out here on the open water then what the hell would it be like on the island itself? It made me want to gag, and suddenly I couldn't bear the idea of staying at this horrible place, away from my friends and the rest of the world, for two weeks.

As we got closer, the island before us looked like it was nothing *but* rock. I couldn't see any trees or flowers or beaches. There were a few stone cairns standing along the clifftop, but otherwise it was just jagged rocks and pale wings.

The boat drew closer and closer, and we soon spotted the gannets wheeling above us in the sky. They were startlingly huge – as big as geese – and I saw a few of them plunge down into the water head first with unbelievable speed. I'd never seen any bird move that fast before, and their shimmering white shapes beneath the rippling water looked strangely like human hands grasping for the surface. The birds' raucous calls were loud, persistent and grating, and again I wondered how I would ever be able to stand two weeks here.

Eventually the island loomed directly above us, and I saw that Jim was right. The soaring cliffs only appeared white because of the thousands of birds perched on them. I'd never seen so many in one place before, and it was quite unnerving. The smell was even stronger up close, and I really thought I might gag. And there was the lighthouse. Impossible to miss, it balanced right on the edge of the clifftop, reaching straight and tall into the sky.

There was something odd about the way it stood so very still when surrounded by the constant motion of the ocean and the birds. My seasickness had eased a little now, but the contrast made me feel a bit queasy again and I found I wanted to look anywhere but at the lighthouse.

I'd hoped for some kind of pier, but no such luck. Jim just navigated the boat into a little inlet – the only one on the island apparently – and Rosie and I had to leap over the side into ankle-deep water. I could see now why Dad had ordered us to travel light and was glad I'd only brought a backpack.

"See you in two weeks," Jim said, already guiding the boat back out, as if he couldn't leave

Bird Rock fast enough.

No one was waiting for us. Dad had said in his message that as he couldn't know exactly what time we'd arrive we should just go straight to the lighthouse. So Rosie and I picked our way across the beach. We had to climb a steep hill littered with stones to reach the clifftop. I kept a close eye on Rosie, alert for any signs of fatigue, but she seemed perfectly fine now that we were off the boat.

The island was a barren, ugly place, and the stink from the birds was absolutely unbearable. All that muck attracted flies too; their irritating buzzing was noticeable even above the pounding of the sea against the cliffs. The birds themselves were everywhere and turned their heads to stare at us coldly as we walked by. They had extremely pale eyes, with just a single black dot of a pupil that almost looked as if it had been painted on. Their grey beaks were razor sharp.

We rounded a corner and all of a sudden the lighthouse rose before us, with the keeper's cottage attached to one side. It was extremely tall – hundreds of metres at least – and just the thought of being in the room at the top set off my vertigo and made my knees feel shaky.

Up close, it was in a worse state than I'd realized. Dad's email had said that the building had been recently restored, but the tired old paint was peeling from the exterior, and the windows were dark and dirty. Some of the wooden shutters on the upper levels were hanging from their hinges.

Rosie seemed thoroughly delighted and was already reaching for her phone. "This is perfect!" she exclaimed, snapping a picture.

"Shouldn't you be using your digital camera?" I asked. "Surely a ghost would be much easier to photoshop in later that way?"

Rosie stuck her tongue out at me. "It came out all blurry anyway."

I glanced at her screen and got a brief glimpse of the lighthouse photo before Rosie pressed delete.

"Let's go and take a look," I said, very much hoping it was better inside.

We walked over to the front door and pushed it open.

Chapter Three

Watery sunlight filtered through the windows of a large entrance hall with wooden floorboards. We could see doors leading off to other rooms, and there was a spiral staircase over to the left, which I guessed must lead up into the lighthouse itself. Beneath the ever-present bird smell, I could detect salt, damp and woodsmoke. A lone fly droned loudly somewhere up near the ceiling.

A large wooden table on the opposite wall took up much of the room, and there was a clutter of rulers, callipers, notebooks and various other ornithologist's equipment spread across it. There was also a letter propped against a lantern. Rosie walked over to pick it up, and I went to peer over her shoulder. I knew at once that the handwriting wasn't Dad's, which meant that it must be Kate's.

Dear Rosie and Jess,

Welcome to Bird Rock! I hope you had a pleasant journey and are excited to settle into your new home! We're certainly delighted to have you here. Depending on what time you arrive, you hopefully won't have too long to wait until we return from our birdwatching, but in the meantime please explore the lighthouse — it's quite fascinating. There's some food in the fridge for lunch — do help yourselves.

We look forward to seeing you soon.

Lots of love,

Kate, Dad and Charlie xxxx

I wrinkled my nose. It still rankled that Dad had another family. One he seemed to prefer to us. One he saw every day rather than for a few miserable weeks out of the year. He'd visited more regularly back when Rosie had been ill, but now we just saw him in the summer holidays. Part of me wondered whether he'd even remembered we were coming today, or if Kate had had to remind him about all the practical stuff — writing notes, making up beds, leaving lunch.

Rosie put down the letter and pushed open the nearest door to reveal a large kitchen. A scrubbed wooden table sat at one end, and there was a fridge and a stove, as well as a big, open stone fireplace. A log basket was piled high in the corner, and I guessed the cold ashes were the source of the woodsmoke I'd smelled on the way in. A couple of threadbare sofas were positioned round the fireplace, and a clunky-looking radio sat on the worktop. There were big baskets of white candles on the mantelpiece and dribbly stubs in holders scattered throughout the room.

We walked in and startled another couple of large, fat flies. They began to drone sluggishly against the window, looking for a way out. When I opened the window to try to shoo them away, two more flew in instead, so I gave up and slammed the window closed with a bang. There were several cans of fly spray around, and the smell of it hung faintly in the air. I could see dead flies on the floor too. Then my eye fell on another note from Kate, lying on the work surface.

No kettle, I'm afraid, but you can heat water in a saucepan on the hob, and there's tea and coffee in the cupboard. Use bottled water, not from the tap xx

I rolled my eyes. "Why didn't one of them think to pack a kettle?"

I rummaged in the cupboards until I found a saucepan. Everything in the kitchen felt sticky – the cupboard handles, the window latches, the knobs on the hob. It was like salt had blown in from the ocean and settled over everything. There was bottled water on the worktop so I put it on to boil and saw that Rosie was checking her phone.

"Any service?" I asked without much hope as I took two mugs down from the cupboard.

"Nope." Rosie shoved it back in her pocket. "No bars at all."

We just about had time for a cup of tea and a quick sandwich before the front door opened and everyone arrived in a flurry of activity. Rosie and I went to the doorway to see Dad and Kate putting down their equipment while Charlie kicked off his boots.

"Girls!" Dad exclaimed. "It's so good to see you!"

Dad was tall, with brown hair, whereas Kate was petite, with hair so dark it was almost black.

42

They were both flushed and windswept from the walk back. Beside them, little Charlie looked just as he did in Dad's Facebook photos – dark hair like Kate's, a smattering of freckles and the cheekiest grin I'd ever seen. While Dad and Kate were still shrugging off their windbreakers, Charlie came racing over to stare up at us with an expectant expression on his face.

"Um, hi?" I said.

"Hi!" he replied. "I'm Charlie! I like snails and tractors."

"Oh. That's cool," I said. He seemed to expect more of a reply, so I added, "I like … um … books and stars."

Charlie turned his gaze on Rosie, who smiled at him.

"I like crystals and photography," she said.

"Cool! I made you this!" He produced a battered piece of paper from his pocket and handed it to me. "I have to go and check on my snail friends now. Bye!"

And before I could reply, he went zooming off up the stairs.

"Sorry about Charlie," Kate said. "He's going

through a shy phase, so he might not say much until he gets used to you."

I assumed she was joking and looked down at the paper Charlie had given me. It was a crayon drawing of the lighthouse stretching up into a sky filled with dozens of birds. Wavy lines formed a grey sea that lapped at the rocks. And lined up before the lighthouse were a family of stick figures that I guessed were meant to represent us: Dad, Kate, Charlie, Rosie and me – all holding hands. Underneath, Charlie had written:

DeAr Rosey aNd JeSS,
WeLcomE to BIRD ROCK!
LoVe CHARLIE Xxxx

I put the drawing in my pocket and Dad came over to give us both a hug. These first meetings always felt awkward, and it was even worse with Kate hovering there, obviously unsure of whether she should hug us too. Finally, to my relief, she decided on a wave and a bright smile. "Welcome to the lighthouse," she said. "Was the journey OK?"

"Er, no, it was rubbish," I replied, turning a scowl

on Dad. "Why didn't you warn us about the boat trip?"

He looked baffled. "What, didn't you enjoy it?" he asked. "We thought it was marvellous fun. Charlie had the time of his life. He's been very excited about your arrival. I'm afraid it's been rather boring for him here with us over the last three days."

"Is he OK with all the birds?" I asked. "And the cliffs? There aren't even any rails."

"Oh, he's fine," Dad said. "He's been coming on research trips with us since he was tiny, and he's always so well-behaved. We never have any problems with him." He gave a small chuckle. "He's nothing like I was at that age, that's for sure. Shall we sit down for a cup of tea? And then we'll give you a tour of the lighthouse. It's an amazing building."

Amazing wasn't the word I'd have used, but we all trooped back into the kitchen and were soon sitting round the table with steaming mugs in front of us.

"I thought you said in your email that this place had been restored?" I asked, not really caring that obvious irritation had crept into my tone.

"It has," Dad replied. "You should have seen it before. Bits of the ceiling were falling down. And there wasn't any electricity."

I wrinkled my nose. "But it's so…" The word I wanted to use was *icky*. "It feels really tired and old, Dad."

He shrugged. "That's hardly surprising. The lighthouse was built in 1807. At least the exterior and the keeper's cottage were. It's thought that the lighthouse itself is about a hundred years older than that. It was getting to the point that it needed strengthening, and they decided the best way to do so was to build another lighthouse around it. So it's really a tower within a tower, which is kind of cool."

"There's a weed growing through the crack in that flagstone." I pointed. "Everything's sticky with salt, and there are flies everywhere."

"The flies are a nuisance but it's impossible to keep them out, I'm afraid," Dad said with a sigh. "You open the windows and more of them just come buzzing in. They're attracted by the birds, you see. It's probably best to keep the windows and doors closed as much as possible so that the gannets don't try to fly in. As for the rest of your complaints, well, we're on an island in the middle of the North Atlantic. Permanently buffeted by the elements. Nothing stays pristine here forever."

"I never said that I wanted everything to be *pristine*," I replied, annoyed that he was already twisting my words and trying to make me sound unreasonable. "But it would be nice if the rooms weren't full of flies and weeds."

I tried not to think about all the fun stuff I was missing out on with my friends back home for this, but it was hard not to feel a rush of irritation towards Dad. If he really wanted to see us, was it too much to ask him to come to London as usual rather than dragging us out to the middle of nowhere?

"Try to think of it as 'rustic'," Kate suggested in a maddeningly cheerful tone.

I gritted my teeth to stop myself from snapping something rude at her.

"Is there a TV?" Rosie asked.

"Nope, just the radio." Dad indicated to the one on the worktop. "You can listen to music in the kitchen if you're lucky enough to find a signal, but don't take it out and about with you – it's literally our lifeline to the outside world. We brought a backup too, but it was damaged during the boat trip. Without this radio, we've no other way of communicating with the mainland. We've got a set of walkie-talkies, but they don't have much of a range."

"Well, it'll still be fun to explore the island," Rosie said with a beseeching glance at me.

"I guess it's not every day you have a whole island to yourself," I agreed, trying to find a positive for my sister's sake.

"About that," Dad said. "We won't exactly have it to ourselves after all. I'm afraid we'll be sharing it with some guga hunters."

I frowned. "What's a guga hunter?"

"It's an ancient Hebridean tradition," Kate explained. "Every year in August, ten people from the nearest island come to stay on Bird Rock for two weeks to hunt the guga. That's the Scottish Gaelic name for young gannets. It's outlawed in the rest of the UK, but this hunt has a special licence that allows them to continue." She sounded disapproving. "It's one of the things your father and I hope to change with our research. Guga meat is considered a delicacy, and the hunters are allowed to catch up to two thousand birds a year."

"They're scheduled to arrive tomorrow," Dad said. "Perhaps you saw them when you were there? Anyway, now our visits are overlapping. The hunters will be staying in the stone bothies on the other side of the island."

He gave me a wry smile. "If you think things are basic here, Jess, just imagine what it's like in those bothies the monks built. They're literally stone huts, with no facilities, or running water, or anything. The hunters have got campfires and sleeping bags, and that's about it. The hunt isn't a pretty sight, by the way – the birds get their heads bashed open on the rocks, so I'd stay well away."

He stood up. "Come on, let's show you around. You'll like it here once you've had the chance to settle in. Most people only ever view Bird Rock from the water, so it really is a once-in-a-lifetime opportunity to be able to stay on an island like this."

I was thinking it was an opportunity I'd rather not have had, but before I could say a word there was a loud knock at the front door.

We all paused. Dad had just said there was no one else on the island at the moment.

"It's probably Charlie," Kate suggested, but as she spoke we heard our half-brother come clattering down the stairs to throw open the door.

"Hello!" His bright little voice rang out clearly from the hall. "I'm Charlie. Who are you?"

Chapter Four

We all hurried from the kitchen in time to hear the visitor speak. "Are your parents here?"

To my surprise, the boy from the hostel was standing on the doorstep, wearing a jacket with a little silver football badge on the pocket. His eyes flicked to me, then narrowed in confusion for a moment before recognition filled them.

"Wait, I know you! You're that girl who was laughing at my dad in the hostel."

"I wasn't *laughing* at him—" I began, my face already growing hot.

"Whatever." He waved my words away and looked straight past me at Dad and Kate. "My name's Will. I'm one of the guga hunters."

"Oh, so you arrived a day early?" I saw a stiffness

come into Dad's shoulders. "I'm Doctor Nathan Oliver, but I suppose you know that already."

He held out his hand, but Will didn't take it. "You have to leave," he said.

"Now listen, young man," Dad said, dropping his hand and using his gruff, no-nonsense tone. "I don't know why you're here, but we're not leaving Bird Rock. We'll just have to share this island for the next two weeks. I hope that we can keep out of one another's way. If you don't disturb our work, then I promise we won't disturb yours either."

"No." Will shook his head and took a step forward. "You don't understand. I mean you can't be *here*. In the lighthouse."

Dad stared at him. "I beg your pardon?"

"There's something wrong with it." Will's jaw tightened. "I know how this sounds, but you need to listen. The lighthouse is haunted. Cursed. It's a dangerous place. Something will happen if you stay here. Something bad—"

"That's enough." Dad sounded suddenly angry. "We've already been here for three days, and apart from some irritating flies it's been perfectly fine. If you think some old ghost story is going to unsettle us, then you're mistaken. Now please go back to the other hunters. I don't want to see you hanging around here again."

Will shook his head, a bleak look in his eyes. "When things start to go wrong – and at some point they will – please think about what I said. And radio for a boat at once. Don't delay. Just get yourselves off this island. Before it's too late."

And with that he turned and began to walk slowly down the path leading to the cliff. Dad closed the door on him firmly and looked back at us with a forced smile.

"Well," he said, "I told you there might be tensions with the guga hunters. It's a shame we couldn't have come to the island after they'd left, but there we are. I think it's best that you steer clear of them."

"He was talking about the missing keepers," Rosie said, unable to keep the excitement from her voice. "Wasn't he?"

"Well, there is a bit of a story attached to the lighthouse," Dad replied. "It's an urban legend – like the *Mary Celeste*."

I glanced at Charlie, wondering if he was spooked by any of this, but he looked pleased.

"Some of the keepers who worked here went *maaaaaad*," he announced.

"Charlie!" Kate frowned. "We've talked about this. Those men were unwell. They had breakdowns, but people didn't know much about mental health back in those days. We understand a lot more now. There's really nothing to worry about, so please don't cry."

But Charlie wasn't crying – in fact, he still looked delighted.

"The Scottish Seabird Centre want to increase their income by running boat tours to some of the more remote islands," Dad went on. "So tourists can see the birds up close and so on. I guess they figured that if they made more of the lighthouse mystery then it would be an even bigger draw. They're actually in the middle of collating some of the lighthouse's paperwork to eventually create displays here for the tourists. Logbooks, telegrams, newspaper clippings, that kind of thing."

Kate sighed. "That hunter's got Charlie all upset. You go on with the tour – I'm going to take him off for some quiet time. Sorry, girls, he's just a bit sensitive about these things."

I assumed Kate was just trying to get out of joining us, perhaps to give us some alone time with Dad or something. She went upstairs with Charlie, and Dad suggested we might like to see the remains of the old keeper's garden. The three of us traipsed outside.

There wasn't much to see – just a few crumbling old walls and long-barren vegetable patches. I suspected that he'd really brought us outside so he could check that Will had gone. Sure enough, as soon as Dad saw his figure retreating down the cliff path, he tried to lead the way back in, but my eye was caught by something at the base of the tower.

"What's that?" I asked, walking over to it.

"That? Oh, it's just a memorial. To one of the keepers who used to work here."

It was a plain wooden cross with a brass plaque fastened to it. The engraved words read: JOHN PORTER. REST IN PEACE.

I nudged Rosie. "Perhaps a good place to take some photos at night," I said. "In case his ghost comes out to haunt the grave."

"It's not a grave, stupid," Rosie replied.

"Well, the cross could still make for a spooky photo," I said.

"What's all this about spooky photos?" Dad asked.

I felt a flare of irritation towards him, like I always did when he asked questions like this. If he was even the tiniest bit involved in our lives, then he would know what kind of stuff Rosie was into. She didn't seem to mind, though, and eagerly told him about the competition.

"Now I'm with you," Dad said. "Well, I can't say I've seen anything strange here yet, but perhaps you'll have more luck with that camera of yours. As long as the ghosts aren't camera-shy, of course."

The jokey way he spoke made it clear that he didn't think for a moment there were any ghosts here. Will had definitely been barking up the wrong tree with Dad – he had the same complete lack of superstition that I did. We went inside and Dad waved towards a door in the hall that he said led to a basement.

"Nothing much to see down there except an old generator and a lot of dead spiders," he told us, before leading on.

My heart sank as we went through the rooms. The entire lighthouse smelled dank, and there were flies buzzing about *everywhere*. The cottage itself wasn't large. Apart from the kitchen and living room, there was a bathroom on the ground floor and one bedroom, which Dad and Kate were using. The other two bedrooms were upstairs. One of them belonged to Charlie, and the other, Dad told us, was for Rosie and me. Dad seemed to expect us to be annoyed about having to share, but Rosie didn't mind, and I was secretly pleased. Ever since her illness, I'd felt like I couldn't have Rosie too close to me. It was hard to let go of that nagging fear that she might suddenly be snatched away.

"We didn't think you'd want to share with Charlie," Dad was saying, "since he snores in his sleep. Sleepwalks sometimes too."

He opened the door, and I saw that the room had an incredible view, with the windows looking directly out on to the sea. But other than that it was a bit depressing. There weren't even any beds – just a blow-up mattress on the floor with a couple of sleeping bags and pillows.

"It's a bit basic, Dad," I ventured.

"Well, yes, I suppose it is a little," he replied. "But if you can cope with camping then I thought this would be doable too."

"I hate camping," I said through gritted teeth. Sometimes I couldn't help wondering whether Dad knew anything about Rosie and me at all.

"We should bring some candles in from the kitchen, just in case the power cuts out," Dad said cheerfully, as if I hadn't even spoken. "It happens sometimes, especially if the weather's bad, which it frequently is here."

"You're really selling the place," I said sarcastically. "Sounds amazing."

I thought Dad might tell me off for being cheeky, but instead he looked suddenly hurt and a bit tired. "Please, Jess," he said. "Just … give it a chance? You never know, you might end up having a good time here."

Rosie reached out and squeezed my arm briefly. I could feel her willing me not to be moody and spoil things, so I forced myself to smile, even though it felt wrong, like wearing a mask.

"Fine. I'll try."

Dad beamed. "Good. So that's it – you've seen everything."

"What about the rest of the lighthouse?" Rosie asked. She gestured to where the spiral staircase continued up to a trapdoor above us.

"Oh, it's just some maintenance rooms up there," Dad said. "And the lantern room itself, of course. It's all off limits. The trapdoor's chained up. That part hasn't been restored yet, so it's probably not safe. We'll give you some time to get settled in. Kate and I have got a few things to finish up this afternoon, so perhaps you might like to explore the island a bit before it gets dark? Maybe take Charlie with you. Get to know each other."

Dad went back downstairs without waiting for a response. Since there was no wardrobe or other storage, it seemed a bit pointless unpacking, but Rosie wanted to get out the crystals she'd brought with her.

"They need cleansing in the sun or moonlight," she said, carefully lining them up on the windowsill. "To recharge their energy."

I resisted the urge to roll my eyes and went to freshen up in the bathroom. It was an odd space, built into the turret of the lighthouse itself, so the walls were spherical. I'd never been in a perfectly circular room before, and the effect was weirdly unsettling – it felt unnatural for there to be no corners.

The windows were tiny and dirty, meaning I had to turn the light on even though it was the middle of the day. Big, exposed copper pipes ran along the ceiling, and there was a shower, toilet, bathtub and small basin. I cringed at the sight of the bath. It was rusty and there were little dead bugs in it. I'd definitely be using the shower.

The mirror above the sink was ancient looking, as if it had been in the lighthouse a really long time. Its square corners looked odd against the curved walls, and the glass was so distorted by age that I could hardly make out my reflection – everything appeared warped and out of focus. Surely that was why – just for a moment – it suddenly looked as if the mirror was filled with hands. Dozens and dozens of them, pressing up against one another, their fingers pale against the glass. I blinked, and the hands melted away into smears and scuffs instead. An odd optical illusion but still – it made me catch my breath. Probably thanks to Rosie and all her talk of ghosts.

I shook my head and splashed some water on my face, wincing at how grimy and dirty the taps felt. When I flushed the toilet, the pipes overhead made such a loud noise that I actually jumped. I knew it was just the water rushing through them, but for a moment it really sounded like a person groaning...

I was glad to leave the bathroom and return to our bedroom where Rosie was still tinkering with her crystals, rearranging them on the windowsill. I automatically reached for my phone before remembering I wouldn't be able to scroll through anything without getting online. So I took out the drawing Charlie had given us instead. Now that I looked at it more closely, I realized that there was something odd about it. The stick-people family ought to have goofy smiles on their wonky faces, but instead every one of us had a big, miserable frowny face, as if we all hated being at the lighthouse. Or hated being with each other. Or perhaps hated something that we didn't even know was happening to us just yet.

Not only that but for the first time I noticed there was a sixth person in the drawing. A blurry face peered out from the window right at the very top of the lighthouse. I wondered why Charlie had added it.

"Have you finished faffing around with those

crystals yet?" I asked, putting the weird drawing aside. "We should find Charlie and go for this walk."

"Do you think there might be a lighthouse keeper's uniform around here?" Rosie asked, as she slung her camera strap over her neck. "I could make Dad dress up in it and pose him next to that cross beside the lighthouse, with the sea in the background. It would be perfect for the competition."

"A bit obvious, though, don't you think?" I asked. "Surely no one would fall for that?"

"Maybe you're right," Rosie said, looking thoughtful. "Perhaps something a bit more subtle is better."

She came to join me, and we went to Charlie's bedroom. The door was open, and we could see his stuff scattered everywhere – comics, toys, clothes and books, all thrown into random corners. There was so much of it that it looked like two boys were staying here rather than only one. Rosie raised her camera and snapped a picture. Charlie had been leaning over a small glass tank in one corner, but when he heard the camera go off he immediately darted over to grab us by the hand and drag us across the room.

"Come and meet my snails!" he said excitedly. "I've got six. I found them on the island, and Mummy says I can keep them while we're here as long as I'm really careful to look after them properly, and be gentle, and promise to set them free when it's time to go home."

He pointed into the tank where six little snails were nestled among various twigs and leaves. "This one is Turbo because he's the fastest," he said. "And the others are Rocko, Brian, Winston, Eric and Matilda."

He looked up at us, beaming.

"Great," I managed to say.

"Do you want to have a picnic with my snails?"

"Er … maybe later," I said. "Dad thought you might like to come for a walk with us this afternoon. Perhaps you could show us the island?"

I'd barely finished the sentence before he'd snatched up his binoculars and was zooming off to get his shoes. Rosie and I followed him down to the front door and then made our way along the cliff path. There were loads of gannets – swarming in the air above us, poking about at the edge of the paths, perched upon the stone cairns and diving towards the ocean with that unsettling speed we'd seen from the boat.

I didn't usually have a problem with birds, but I found the sight of these ones a bit unnerving. There were just *so* many. Thousands and thousands. I'd never seen such a large number in one place before. But Dad was an ornithologist after all, so I told myself that he would know if they were dangerous. The smell was disgusting, and flies crawled thickly over every rock. Their constant droning was giving me a headache.

"I've never seen so many flies!" I exclaimed, batting my hand through a cloud of them.

"They come for the bird poo," Charlie said. "Gannets eat loads of fish and squid, and Mummy says that what goes in must come out, and that's why it stinks so much."

We were a short distance from the lighthouse when Charlie paused to raise his binoculars to his eyes and peer out at the horizon.

"I'm looking for sea monsters," he informed us. "There have been hundreds and hundreds of them spotted around Scotland."

"Well, if you keep looking, I'm sure you'll see one,"

Rosie said encouragingly. "There was an article about the Loch Ness monster in the magazine I subscribe to. Some cool new photos have just been published of it."

"Some cool new fakes more like," I muttered.

Rosie ignored me and spoke to Charlie instead. "I'll show you when we get back, if you like?"

He looked delighted. "Awesome!"

While he searched the sea for monsters, Rosie raised her camera and pointed it back at the lighthouse. There was a sharp click as the shutter came down.

"I wouldn't do that if I were you."

We all jumped and turned to see Will sitting on a nearby rock with his elbows on his knees. He'd been so still in the shadows that I hadn't noticed him.

"Do what?" Rosie asked.

"Take photos of the lighthouse," he said, rising slowly to his feet. "It doesn't like it."

Chapter Five

"What do you mean?" Rosie asked, looking eager rather than afraid. "I'm Rosie, by the way, and that's Charlie and Jess. So what's wrong with the lighthouse?"

"Hard to say," Will replied. "Some people believe it was cursed by the Blue Men of the Minch. If you're from London, then I guess you won't have heard of them, but they're—"

"I know who they are," Rosie interrupted, eager to show off her encyclopaedic knowledge of all things weird and wonderful. "They're strange blue men who live in the sea round the Outer Hebrides and cause storms and try to drown people."

Will looked surprised. "That's right."

"You don't honestly believe in things like that,

do you?" I asked, incredulous.

"It doesn't matter what I do or don't believe," he said. "All I know is that there are no records for the original lighthouse's construction. None at all. No architectural plans, no expense accounts, no work schedules or contracts, no deed of ownership, nothing. I know because I've checked. The earliest records that exist relate to when the new tower was built around the old one in the 1800s. But as for the original lighthouse, it's as if nobody knows how it first came to be here, or who built it, or why. No one wants to claim it as their own."

I shrugged. "So what? Paperwork like that must go missing all the time."

"But it doesn't," Will replied. "The lighthouse boards have always been meticulous about that kind of thing. There are records going back hundreds and hundreds of years. A total lack of information isn't just unusual, it's unheard of. There are no references to this one in the archives at all before 1807 when the new tower was built. And no one in authority wants to talk about the lighthouse on Bird Rock."

I didn't see what the big deal was about a bit of missing paperwork and was about to say so when

Will looked at Charlie and said, "How old are you anyway? Like, five?"

"I'm six!" Charlie said, sounding slightly offended. "Six and a half."

Will shook his head. "Mad," he said under his breath. "I never thought the whole family would be here. Six-year-olds. Jesus."

"But why does all that mean we shouldn't take photos of the lighthouse?" Rosie asked.

I could tell she was disappointed with Will's explanations so far – they were nowhere close to being spooky or interesting enough for her.

Will paused, then said, "The Northern Lighthouse Board used to receive dozens of photos of the lighthouse every year. People sent the negatives too."

Rosie raised an eyebrow. "Why?"

"To get the bad luck to stop. The lighthouse doesn't like being photographed." A faint frown line appeared between his eyes. "I don't think it really likes to be seen at all."

"It's a lighthouse," I protested. "It can't *like* or *dislike* anything."

Will shook his head. "But that's where you're wrong. People have died there. Seen things. And if

68

you stay, then something will happen to you too—"

Charlie had looked more fascinated than unnerved up until this point, so I was surprised when he suddenly started to cry – and not just a bit of a sniffle but actual sobbing.

"I don't want to stay in the lighthouse!" he wailed. "I hate it there – I hate it!"

I rolled my eyes at Will. "Thanks a lot," I said. "I'm sure my dad will be really impressed when we take him home like this."

Will shrugged and didn't even try to apologize. He was clearly a bit of an arsehole.

I went to crouch in front of my brother. "It's all right, Charlie. Will was only joking. The lighthouse isn't really haunted. Come on, let's go and see the rest of the island."

To my relief, Will didn't try to stop or follow us, and we left him standing alone on the path. Charlie continued to cry and sniffle for a bit, but then Rosie got him on to the subject of snails and he seemed to calm down and eventually forget about the unpleasant conversation with Will.

Once Charlie had settled, we carried on exploring the island. It wasn't large. I guess you'd walk across it in an hour or so. Which meant that you couldn't go far before you found evidence of the other guga hunters. We saw the bothies perched on the hillside first – the little stone houses built all those years ago by the monks. I had to admit they made the lighthouse look almost homely by comparison. The dark stone huts didn't even have any doors or windows, only gaping holes in the rock for the wind to whistle through. There were several people in windbreakers busying themselves carrying bags back and forth and dragging great lengths of rope.

"Come on," I said at last. "Let's go on before they see us."

We spotted a couple of baby gannets in their nests as we walked, and the thought of their fluffy white heads being bashed open on the rocks made me feel ill. I was glad that Dad's research might help end the hunt. We explored a little more, but there was nothing on the island except birds and flies and the tall stone cairns. It was massively depressing. Finally we looped round to make our way back. Along the way, we noticed several other types of birds among the gannets, and Charlie could name every one.

"That's a guillemot," he said, pointing. "That's a shag. The one by the big rock is a razorbill. And the one back there is a fulmar."

"Oh, look, and there's a snail."

I pointed it out, but to my surprise he said, "Yuck, I hate snails! They're all slimy!"

"What? I thought you—" But Charlie had already scampered off ahead.

It makes my head ache to try to write about Charlie and the snails now.

"Hey, don't go too close to the edge!" I called after him.

Some of the sea cliffs must have been over sixty metres high. I hoped Dad was right and that Charlie wouldn't stray from the path. Now that we'd seen the whole island, I realized that it wasn't the safest place to wander freely about, especially if the rocks were wet and slippery. I'd have to keep an eye on Rosie too, to make sure she didn't start doing anything stupid in order to get the perfect photograph. I hated Bird Rock already, and the two-week trip suddenly seemed to stretch on forever and ever. The sooner we could get off this stinking island and go home, the better.

Before dinner, Dad and Kate explained that once the sun went down the doors needed to be kept closed and so did all the shutters, or else the lights could mess things up for people navigating at sea. Rosie and I gave them a hand with the shutters, which, like everything else, were caked in salt. I could even taste it on my lips as I walked back towards the front door. I met Rosie coming the other way and noticed she was frowning.

"What's up?" I asked.

"I think I just saw Charlie in one of the tower windows," she said.

"The tower? But isn't it locked?"

"Maybe he managed to find a key from somewhere?"

Rosie asked him about it at dinner that night, but Charlie just shook his head and looked solemn. "You're not allowed in the tower," he said quietly, almost in a whisper. "It's not safe."

Our brother had seemed quiet and subdued since we sat down at the table. He kept fidgeting in his chair, had hardly touched his dinner and even looked a little pale. He hadn't mentioned seeing Will, but I was afraid he was thinking about the things the guga hunter had told us, and that it was only a matter of time before Charlie started saying he was afraid of the lighthouse again.

"Perhaps it was a gannet you saw," Dad suggested.

Rosie rolled her eyes. "I know the difference between a gannet and a boy, Dad."

"A reflection then," Dad said with a shrug.

Rosie looked unconvinced. "Is there a key to the padlock on that trapdoor here in the building?" she asked.

"I don't think so," Dad replied. "I expect it's back at the lighthouse board."

"Mummy!" Charlie suddenly piped up loudly. "Please may I be excused?"

"Not until you've eaten your dinner," Kate replied.

Charlie stared down miserably at his untouched plate. "But I'm not hungry, Mummy!" He was squirming about in his chair, as if he needed the toilet.

"That's what you said last night, and the night before," Kate said. "I can't think what's got into you – normally you have the appetite of a small horse!" She peered at him. "You don't feel poorly, do you?"

Charlie shook his head. "I don't like this room," he said. "It's sticky. And it smells like fishes. Can I go to my bedroom to see my snails?"

"Afterwards, darling," Kate said in a firm voice. "But first you'll eat at the table with everyone else."

Charlie seemed to give up and began to spoon food into his mouth. In between swallowing, he kept leaning down to peer under the table. When Kate finally asked what he was doing, he looked guilty and said, "I thought there was someone down there. I heard them scratching."

"There's no one under the table, Charlie," Kate replied with endless patience. "Concentrate on your food, please."

"Did you manage to take some photos this afternoon?" Dad asked Rosie.

She nodded but didn't get the chance to say anything before Charlie piped up again. "Rosie took a photo of the lighthouse, and Will says that it's *cursed*."

I silently groaned.

"What's this?" Dad said, sounding exasperated. "Did you talk to that boy again?"

"We just ran into him—" I began.

"Well, if that happens again, then walk away at once, please," Dad said, frowning at me. "He's obviously out to make trouble, and I don't want him filling your heads with a lot of stupid nonsense about the lighthouse."

I was a bit annoyed by Dad's tone. It felt like I was being scolded for something that wasn't my fault.

The conversation around the table was stilted until Dad tried to lighten the mood by asking me if I'd brought my binoculars for stargazing. I was about to reply when my eyes fell on the window, and the words lodged in my throat.

There was a pair of white hands pressed flat against the glass.

Someone was out there, standing on the other side of the window, yet I couldn't make out anything of the person themselves. Just their hands. Unlike the cloudy image in the bathroom mirror, these hands looked startlingly clear and pale against the darkness of the night – too white to belong to any living person. I took a sharp intake of breath, my heart suddenly racing. But before I could say anything, the hands vanished.

"Jess?" Dad said. "Are you OK?"

I glanced back at the table and noticed that Charlie was missing. He must have slipped away unnoticed and gone outside. I breathed a sigh of relief. Still … the memory of what I'd just seen at the window was imprinted on the inside of my eyelids. There was nothing outright horrifying about the hands, especially now that I knew they must belong to Charlie, but somehow the image was unsettling, and I could still feel my skin prickling with unease.

"I'm fine," I said in response to Dad's question. "I just saw someone at the window. I think Charlie must be out there."

Kate sighed. "I wish he wouldn't sneak off like that."

I hadn't really meant to dob him in, but it didn't seem all that safe for him to be outside by himself in the dark.

"Well, I'm finished with dinner too, so is it all right if I go?" I asked.

"Sure," Dad replied.

It had been a long and disappointing day, and I ached to be by myself for a bit. I went upstairs and rummaged through my bag for my binoculars.

As I buttoned up my coat, I heard Charlie's piping voice from next door.

"But I *wasn't* outside, Mummy! And I don't *want* any more food!"

I shook my head. I didn't really care that he was lying about being outside. The important thing was that he was back in the lighthouse, meaning I could stargaze in peace. I went downstairs and headed for the door.

"Make sure to lock it behind you when you come in," Dad called. "I don't want Charlie sleepwalking outside."

"OK," I replied.

As soon as I stepped outside, I could feel salt settling on my skin and tasted it on my lips again. It made me feel like I permanently needed a shower. I sat on the remnants of a brick wall in the keeper's garden and waited for my eyes to adjust to the darkness. Here, finally, was the one good thing about being on Bird Rock – the stars were amazing. And as always, their bright white lights helped calm me, made my problems seem small and insignificant. The bird smell was still horrendously bad, but at least the gannets were quieter at night, and so were the flies. The main thing I could hear was the sea, a muffled, hungry roar at the base of the cliffs below.

But then I saw a constellation that shouldn't have been there. My eyes found several stars that together, reated a humanoid shape in the black sky. Only this particular part of the sky wasn't black at all: it was blue, in contrast to the dark all around.

Some people believe it was cursed by the Blue Men of the Minch.

Strange blue men who ... cause storms and try to drown people.

I lowered the binoculars and frowned up at the sky. Brand-new stars didn't simply appear out of nowhere, and in fact now I couldn't see them at all. I shook my head, suddenly feeling a bit dizzy as the stars settled into their usual patterns around me. I must be more tired than I'd thought if I was imagining brand-new constellations. Perhaps it was time to go to bed.

I slipped my binoculars back into their case, then stood up and set off round the base of the tower, towards the front door. I'd forgotten about the memorial cross we'd seen earlier until it suddenly appeared before me, the dark wood shining in a pool of light.

A man stood beside it.

I felt a jolt of shock rush through my body and gave a yelp. After the photo I had suggested to Rosie, for a split second, I almost thought I was looking at the ghost of the dead keeper… But then the man turned, reaching out a hand. "'S all right," he said calmly. "I'm not looking for any trouble. I just thought it best to come at night when there'd be no one else around – or so I thought."

I realized the light was given off by an electric lantern he'd placed on the ground. By its glow, I could see that he was probably in his late forties, with a grey layer of stubble over his jaw, dressed in jeans and a windbreaker. Clearly no ghostly lighthouse keeper.

"Who are you?" I asked.

"Cailean Porter," he said. "I'm one of the guga hunters."

My heart rate slowed a little and I breathed a sigh of relief. "You scared the crap out of me," I said. "What are you doing here?"

"Just leaving some flowers."

He gestured towards the cross and I noticed that there was a small bunch of flowers propped up against it. Something about his lilting accent was reassuring, and I saw that his green eyes were kind, and he looked like someone who smiled often. I felt myself relax.

"John Porter was the last keeper on Bird Rock," Cailean explained. "He was also my grandfather. I always come to pay my respects whenever I'm here. Didn't think anyone would mind if I kept myself to myself."

"Oh. OK."

I glanced at the cross. I'd assumed the man it commemorated had died a hundred or so years ago, so it was odd to think that I was standing beside his grandson. "I didn't realize he was the last keeper here," I said.

"Aye," Cailean replied. "One of a pair anyway. The light was automated soon after that, but I guess a mysterious death would put off most prospective applicants."

"Death?" I asked, startled.

"Sorry. Thought you'd know a bit about the place as you're staying here," Cailean said, watching me closely. "Didn't mean to spook you."

I shrugged. "You didn't," I said. "I mean, it's sad, but I don't believe in ghosts. It's just history."

Cailean looked thoughtful. "Guga hunters are about the least superstitious people you'll ever meet," he said. "You know why?"

I shook my head.

"There's an old sailors' legend that says seabirds are the dead souls of drowned men, and that you bring the worst luck in the world down upon yourself if you hurt one, let alone kill one. But us hunters kill thousands of 'em every time we come to Bird Rock for the harvest. So if any one of us had a superstitious bone in their body, then we wouldn't be coming here to do what we do."

He rubbed the back of his neck. "I'm the same, I reckon," he went on. "Would quite happily walk under a hundred ladders, or open up my brolly indoors, or break a mirror, or anything else you care to mention. One thing I never would do, though, is cross the threshold into that lighthouse."

He looked right at me, the beam from his lantern flickering strangely in his eyes. "It's rotten to the core. And if you lot have any sense, you'll clear out before it can get its poisonous fingers into you." He bent down to scoop up his light. "That's my two pence, for what it's worth."

I crossed my arms over my chest, feeling annoyed that he obviously took me for some impressionable kid who'd be easily frightened.

"Thanks for the tip," I said. "But it's just a building."

"Well, maybe it is and maybe it isnae," he said. "All I know is what my own father told me – that Grandad was the happy, hearty, joyful type, and had been all his life until he came to Bird Rock. Three weeks living in that place, though, and he jumped from the rim of the light."

He glanced past me at the tower looming above us, and I saw in his face that he wasn't trying to scare me – that he honestly believed what he was saying. I couldn't help looking up at the top of the lighthouse too, where the blinding electric light pulsed at intervals. It was so incredibly high up that it was impossible to imagine anyone deliberately jumping from it. Just thinking about it made me feel sick, and I had the sudden urge to move back a few steps, as if I was standing on someone's grave.

"Heck of a mess it was, when the assistant keeper found him," Cailean went on unhelpfully. "The lighthouse did something to him, that's what I believe, and it's what I'll believe until my dying day. So have a care, lassie, that's all. And while we're on that subject ... I noticed you young people earlier on the cliff path. You were talking to Will."

"We ran into him," I replied.

"Well, make sure that you don't," Cailean said. "Run into him, I mean. He's been through a difficult time recently. His sister died at the lighthouse last summer."

"Oh." I was startled to hear this and felt a flash of sympathy for Will. At the same time, I couldn't help being curious about what had happened. There must have been some kind of accident. "I'm sorry."

"Ever since then ... young Will hasn't been himself," Cailean went on. "So just keep your distance, all right?"

I shrugged. "Fine with me."

"Sorry again for the intrusion," Cailean said. "I reckon I've taken up enough of your time, so goodnight to you."

"Goodnight," I replied.

I watched him crunch off along the gravel path into the darkness. I was glad Rosie hadn't been there for that conversation as she'd be unsettled by what had happened to Will's sister. It was the sort of thing that would nag away at her and that she'd spend too long thinking about. Resolving not to say a word to her about what I'd just learned, I went back inside.

Chapter Six

I found Dad and Kate poring over notes they'd taken earlier that day. I didn't say anything about the guga hunter. I knew Dad wouldn't like that Cailean had been out there at this time of night, and I didn't want to get drawn into a big discussion about it or be told off for talking to him.

There was absolutely nothing to do at the lighthouse in the evenings. No TV, no internet, no nothing. I was glad I at least had stargazing to keep me occupied. Charlie had already gone up to bed, and Rosie was in our bedroom, so I went upstairs to join her, only to find that Charlie wasn't asleep after all. He was crouched at the end of the landing, playing with a little wind-up toy that clicked and clacked its way out of the shadows, knocked against my shoe and fell to the floor. I peered down and saw that it was an old-fashioned-looking tin soldier, its arms and legs still jerking stiffly up and down at its sides.

"Charlie, I'm pretty sure you're supposed to be in bed," I said, leaning down to pick up the soldier. "Where did you get this anyway? It looks ancient."

"It's not mine," Charlie replied.

"Whose is it then?" I glanced up and froze. For a weird moment, it looked as if there were two boys lurking in the shadows – Charlie looking straight up at me and a second boy who'd turned to face the wall. But then my eyes adjusted, and I saw that it was only Charlie there.

"It's my friend's," he said with a giggle, snatching it from me and then running off to his own room.

I let him go and went on to the bedroom I was sharing with Rosie. She was reading her magazines, but looked up when I came in.

"It's going to be *soooo* boring here," I said, throwing myself down beside her. I reached over to my bag and grabbed a packet of sweets from the journey, offering them to Rosie before taking one for myself. "I can't believe we spent all those hours travelling only to end up in Scotland. We could have been somewhere really hot and exotic by now."

"I like it here," Rosie said, turning another page of her magazine.

"You would." I sighed. "Seeing as it's both spooky and weird. I'm tired. I'm going to bed."

I gathered up my things and went to the bathroom. The pipes rumbled and creaked overhead once again as I brushed my teeth and got changed into my pyjamas. When I returned to our room, Rosie was still reading her magazine, engrossed in a story about the Bermuda Triangle. I hoped she wasn't going to stay up too much longer because the light was disturbing the bluebottle that had become trapped in there with us. It droned endlessly as it kept up a steady search for an exit, bumping against the walls and shuttered windows, and even buzzing into my hair a few times so that I had to bat it away.

"Goodnight," I said, as I got into my sleeping bag.
"Night."

The blow-up mattress wasn't particularly comfortable, and the pillow smelled damp. I thought the noise from the fly and the things Cailean had told me would keep me awake, but I must have been more worn out than I thought because I fell asleep almost at once.

It was pitch-black when I woke up a little while later. With the shutters barring the windows, there wasn't even the soft glow of moonlight shining through the glass. For a disorienting moment, I wasn't quite sure where I was. But then the distant roar of the sea filtered through to me from outside, and Bird Rock and the lighthouse came flooding back. Everything was fine. I was sleeping on the floor with my sister. I couldn't see her, but I could hear her breathing right beside me.

I realized she must be awake too because at that moment she reached for my hand and gave it a squeeze. It was a bit muggy in the room with no windows open, and Rosie's hand was clammy. I squeezed her hand back, and we stayed like that for a few minutes before I started to get fidgety and wanted to roll over. I tried to extricate my hand, but she tightened her grip – not just a little but a lot.

"Ow! Rosie, cut it out."

I snatched my hand away, but then a voice spoke

from the doorway.

"Did you say something, Jess?"

I looked up, startled, my head suddenly fogged with confusion. Rosie was walking into our bedroom, a torch in her hand. In its light, I could see that the sleeping bag beside me was empty.

"What … weren't you just here?" I was about to add *holding my hand*, but couldn't quite bring myself to say the words.

"I went to get a glass of water," Rosie replied. She came over and climbed into her sleeping bag.

Dreaming. I must have been asleep and dreaming. That was the only explanation.

Rosie lay back down, and I longed to do the same, but my heart was still racing, and I needed to pee anyway. I reluctantly left the warmth of my sleeping bag, trying very hard not to think about that clammy hand squeezing mine tight in the darkness. It had felt so real…

I couldn't remember where the light switches were out on the landing so I groped and fumbled my way down the dark corridor. When I got to the bathroom, I found the electric light and flicked the switch. It came on with a buzzing sound, filling the room with a sickly glow. The room wasn't empty as I'd expected, and I let out a cry of surprise at the sight of Charlie sitting in the bath, his knees pulled up in front of him, staring straight ahead.

"What are you doing?" I yelped. "It's the middle of the night! You're supposed to be in bed."

The next second I recalled what Dad had said about Charlie sleepwalking, but it didn't seem like that was what was happening here. His gaze was perfectly focused as he looked at me.

"I couldn't sleep." Then in a very quiet voice, he added, "There's someone in my room."

"What? No, there isn't."

I was about to send him back to bed when it occurred to me that I probably should check that there *wasn't* anyone in his room. We weren't alone on the island after all – there had been a guga hunter hanging around outside just that evening, a fact that I'd failed to mention to anybody. It would be pretty shitty of me if I sent Charlie back to bed only for him to be snatched away.

"All right, show me," I said with a sigh.

He scrambled out of the bath, tucked his hand into mine and led me back to the landing. This time I was able to find the light switch and flick it on before we went into Charlie's bedroom. His train night light was on, softly illuminating the room, which was completely empty.

"You see?" I said. "No one here."

"He must have gone back upstairs," Charlie replied.

"Now I know you're making it up," I said. "We can't get upstairs – the trapdoor's chained up."

"Not at night," Charlie insisted. "He opens it."

"Would you please just get back into bed and go to sleep?" I asked, trying not to sound too exasperated. This was way more than I wanted to be dealing with in the middle of the night.

Charlie obediently returned to his sleeping bag and snuggled into it. I hesitated in the doorway for a minute, wondering whether there was anything else I ought to do.

"Do you need anything?" I finally asked. "A glass of water from the kitchen?"

"Can I have a ham sandwich?"

I rolled my eyes. "No. It's late. Almost breakfast time. You can have something then."

"OK," he replied in a small voice that immediately made me feel bad.

"Well … goodnight then."

"Goodnight, Jess."

I went back to use the bathroom before returning to the landing. I was just passing the staircase and probably would have walked right past, but I felt a cold draught trail across my skin, like fingers. I shivered slightly and glanced up, thinking there might be a window open nearby.

And that's when I saw it.

The trapdoor leading up to the lighthouse tower was no longer chained up. It was wide open.

Chapter Seven

For a long moment, I just stood and stared at the yawning black hole leading to the top of the tower. What the hell? *How* had it come open? It had been locked with an actual chain. Then my eye fell on something propped against the wrought-iron bannister of the staircase – it was a pair of bolt cutters. And shining on the floor beside it was a little silver football badge – just like the one that had been pinned to Will's jacket. Had he actually been stupid enough to break into the lighthouse tower? And how had he got into the cottage in the first place? Perhaps he was the person Charlie had seen in his bedroom? I hesitated, wondering whether I should go and wake Dad.

But then I remembered how he had specifically

asked me to make sure I locked the door when I came in from stargazing, because of Charlie's sleepwalking. My blood ran cold as I realized I'd forgotten. I hurried downstairs and sure enough, the kitchen door was unlocked. I turned the key in the lock and put it up on the hook before returning to the landing. All thoughts of telling Dad about Will disappeared as then I'd have to explain how he'd got inside the lighthouse in the first place. The easiest thing seemed to be to deal with Will and get him out as quickly and quietly as possible.

So I walked over to the spiral staircase, slipped Will's badge in my pocket, put my foot on the first step and climbed up towards the trapdoor in the ceiling. The metal stairs beyond were cold beneath my bare feet and, like everything else in this place, coated in a layer of sticky salt. It felt weird climbing up into pitch-black, and I stupidly found myself thinking about pale hands reaching out for me in the dark. I *really* had to stop paying attention to talk of ghosts and ghouls. I reminded myself firmly that I didn't believe in any of that stuff. But that did not mean the thought of it wasn't freaky…

It felt cooler and mustier as I climbed, and soon I reached a small landing with a room leading off it. I paused, wondering whether I should investigate, but if Will was there surely he'd have a light on? I continued to climb, up and up. Before long, I'd gone so far that I was almost glad there was no light, as looking down would have been enough to make me break out in a cold sweat. I might not have believed in ghosts, but I *was* afraid of heights. The spiral staircase was so narrow and twisty that it made me feel a bit dizzy. Finally I reached a new level. The door leading off from the landing was closed, but a faint strip of light shone from beneath the gap. There was someone in there.

I stepped on to the wooden boards of the landing, wincing slightly as they gave a loud creak. They were filthy too – I could feel a thick coating of dust beneath my feet. The air up here smelled of saline, corrosion and rusted metal. I straightened my shoulders, marched over to the door and pushed it open. It swung inwards to reveal a small, circular room full of filing cabinets. The square objects looked odd against the curved walls, and I felt a faint prickling ache behind my eyes, as if I was looking at an optical illusion.

On the walls were dozens of photos of the lighthouse. They weren't new pictures but old black-and-white shots, some in frames. They made the room seem like a shrine. There were pieces of paper and leather-bound books scattered all over the floor. And sitting behind an old wooden desk, a large book open before him, was Will.

He was still wearing the same outfit from the day before, which made me very aware of the fact that I was in my pyjamas. They definitely weren't the clothes I'd have chosen if I'd known I was going to be confronting an intruder.

"Don't scream," Will said.

He didn't look at all guilty or startled to be caught out like this. In fact, he was glaring at me, as if *I* was the one who wasn't supposed to be there.

I rolled my eyes. "Why would I scream? I knew it was you up here – I found your badge downstairs." I took it from my pocket and tossed it over to him. "And your bolt cutters. You know you almost frightened my little brother out of his wits! He told me there was someone in his room, but I didn't believe him."

Will frowned. "I didn't go into his room. Why would I? I came straight here."

I shook my head, not believing him. He'd probably ended up in Charlie's room by mistake at some point and just didn't want to admit it.

"Why are you up here?" I asked. "My dad will go nuts if he finds out."

"I wanted to see the old logbooks," Will replied. "From the keepers who worked here. You should look yourself. It's Jess, right? These accounts prove what I've been trying to tell you – that there's something rotten and evil here. That there always has been. Even the first lighthouse keepers were aware of it, back when this place was new."

"You still haven't answered my question," I said impatiently. "If the lighthouse is as dangerous as you say, then why are you here? This is trespassing and criminal damage."

I glanced down at the desk, and a few lines from the nearest logbook jumped out at me.

Porter's been acting strangely again today. Like a different man from the one who arrived on Bird Rock a week ago. Keeps

turning the lighthouse upside down, looking
for something, but when I ask him about
it the craziest thing is he doesn't seem to
know what he's looking for...

With a jolt, I realized that the book was referring to Cailean's grandfather – the keeper who'd fallen to his death. Other words and phrases leaped out at me from the page: *mood swings, vivid nightmares, violent outbursts, Strangers' Room…*

"What's the Strangers' Room?" I asked.

To my surprise, Will flinched. "Don't go into the Strangers' Room," he said sharply.

I raised an eyebrow. "How can I when I don't know what it is?"

"It's here in the lighthouse. You'd know if you went inside," he replied. "It's not like the other rooms. It's… Look, we shouldn't even be talking about it."

"Is that… Is it where your sister died?"

He froze for a moment, and when he finally looked up at me there was such an icy look of anger on his face that I almost took a step back. "What do you know about my sister?" he asked.

"Only … only that she died here," I said.

"Cailean told me."

"Did he now? Well, she didn't die in the Strangers' Room, but she might as well have. She fell from the window up there and landed on the ground below."

The colour drained from my face. I couldn't imagine witnessing something like that. Just the thought of it happening to Rosie made me feel ill. No wonder Will was a bit unhinged and so obsessed with the lighthouse.

"I'm sorry," I said, even though I knew the words were horribly feeble. "What a terrible accident."

There was a hard look in Will's eyes and bitterness in his voice. "It wasn't an accident. And if you don't want the same thing to happen to your sister then listen to my warning and get her out of this place while you still can. Now would you leave me alone? I've got lots of reading to do here. You can try to drag me out if you like, but I'm pretty confident you won't manage it."

After what he'd just told me, it felt wrong to go tell on him to Dad. It wasn't like he was doing any harm there, poring over old documents, and if learning more about the place where his sister had died helped him get some kind of closure then

I wasn't about to interfere with that.

I left him to it, gathering up the chain when I got to the bottom of the ladder and holding it close against myself so that it didn't clink as I tiptoed into my bedroom, where I hid it behind my backpack. Rosie was sound asleep as I slid in next to her.

It was difficult to prevent Will's words from replaying inside my head:

If you don't want the same thing to happen to your sister, then ... get her out of this place while you still can.

I pushed his words away with an effort. It was desperately sad about Will's sister, and if something ever happened to Rosie then I'd probably go a bit nuts too. I wasn't superstitious, but ever since her illness it had been hard to escape the feeling that a long shadow hung over my little sister. That one way or another her time was going to be cut short...

I shook my head. I wouldn't let myself go down that dark path again. Otherwise I'd never get any rest. So I lay back on the mattress, closed my eyes and willed myself to fall asleep.

Chapter Eight

Day Two

When I woke the next morning, I was surprised to find that Rosie had already gone. It was only 8 a.m., and normally she would sleep in until at least ten. I got up, quickly threw on some clothes, then opened the window and pushed back the wooden shutters. Light washed into the room, along with the scent of seaweed and, unfortunately, guano. Another fly buzzed inside before I could close the window.

When I went past Charlie's room, his door was open and he was still tucked up in his sleeping bag, sound asleep. At the staircase, I saw that Will's bolt cutters were gone and the trapdoor was back in place, so I assumed he'd returned to the guga hunters' camp. I went downstairs and the smell of coffee and toast drew me to the kitchen where

Dad and Kate were having breakfast.

"Morning," Dad said. "I hope you slept well?"

I nodded but avoided the question. "Have you seen Rosie?"

"She's outside with Charlie," Kate told me.

"What? Charlie's in bed asleep. I just saw him."

"Oh. He must have gone back to bed then. He was out there earlier."

I could see Rosie through the window, so I let myself out and made my way along the cliff path towards her. She was examining the screen of her camera, but looked up and waved when she saw me.

"You're up early," I said.

"I couldn't sleep," she replied.

"The blow-up mattress isn't very comfortable, is it?" I said.

"No, it wasn't that." She fiddled with her camera strap. "I had a horrible nightmare. About eels. And birds. They were trapped inside the lighthouse, looking for a way out. It's made me feel a bit unsettled since I got up actually. You know those dreams that just make you feel a bit ... weird? Like you're not yourself?"

I noticed that she looked pale and had to resist

the urge to reach out and put my hand against her forehead.

"At least you've got nice weather for photography today," I said, gesturing at the sun sparkling off the blue waves.

But Rosie pulled a face. "Not much good for spooky photography," she pointed out. "I would've preferred dark skies and ominous clouds. Perhaps it will turn overcast a bit later."

She took out her phone to check the weather.

"No signal, remember?" I reminded her.

"Oh yeah." She shook her head. "Habit." Then she frowned at her phone and said, "That's weird."

"What? Have you got a signal?"

"No, it's not that. My lock screen is a photo of the lighthouse."

"So?"

"So I didn't set it."

I shrugged. "You must have pressed something by mistake."

"I guess."

She went into her phone, but then her eyes narrowed. "This doesn't make sense," she said. "It's the photo of the lighthouse I took when we arrived yesterday – the one I deleted because it was all blurry, but now it's back in my library and it's set as my wallpaper too. Look."

She passed me the phone, and I saw that she was right. There the blurred photo was, time-stamped from yesterday.

"Maybe it's a glitch with your phone, or you pressed the wrong button," I said, handing it back with a shrug. My stomach gave a growl and I thought of the toast in the kitchen. "I'm starving. Why don't we go and have breakfast?"

"OK."

Rosie deleted the lighthouse photo, then we went back inside where Kate and Dad were clearing away their plates.

"Hi, girls," Kate said cheerfully. "There's toast and cereal on the side."

"Thanks," I said.

I grabbed a piece of toast for me and one for Rosie.

Dad put a couple of glasses of juice on the table and said, "Listen, we thought we'd skip work today, as you've only just arrived. There isn't all that much to do here, but perhaps we could go out for a picnic lunch? Find a nice spot along the cliffs?"

I knew Dad was trying to make it nice, but I wished he didn't bother. It would have been easier if it had just been the three of us. With Kate and Charlie, it was bound to feel awkward, but I could see that Rosie was pleased that Dad wanted to spend time with us.

"Sounds good," I forced myself to say.

At that moment, there was a creak in the doorway, and Charlie appeared, still wearing his pyjamas.

"Morning, darling," Kate said. "Are you going to have some breakfast?"

But Charlie was already backing away from the door.

"I ate something earlier," he said, before disappearing back up the stairs.

"Perhaps you girls might like to help me organize the food for our picnic?" Dad asked, looking hopeful.

It was obvious that we didn't have a choice, that he wanted this to be bonding time. Rosie looked delighted too, so I knew I had to go along with it. It was going to be a very boring morning – I almost wished that the lighthouse really was cursed.

At lunchtime, we took the picnic and wandered along the cliff path in the opposite direction to the one we'd explored yesterday. It was all just more of the same: sea and scrub, thousands of shrieking birds, tall cairns and endless bloody flies. I could see straight away that having a picnic on Bird Rock wasn't going to work. Perhaps Dad could too now that we were out here, but he didn't want to say so – we'd just have to make the best of it.

We found a little clearing just off the cliff path that Dad said would be the perfect spot, so we spread out the blanket he'd brought and emptied the basket. It was impossible, though. The flies swarmed around us immediately, crawling all over the sandwiches, landing on our bare skin, refusing to be shooed away.

"This is horrible," I said.

"It's not that bad," Dad replied, batting at a fly for the millionth time.

"I like it!" Charlie insisted.

He certainly seemed to have rediscovered his appetite. He fell on the food like a starved wolf cub. The rest of us were struggling to eat at all with the flies buzzing around. Then the feathers came – dozens and dozens of them, swirling in the air. I couldn't

106

work out where they were coming from at first, but we noticed that a few of the guga hunters had set up a work area on the hill sloping above us.

A load of dead birds lay in a heap near them, and I shuddered when I spotted that they'd all had their heads removed, leaving only long, dangly necks that flopped about in a disturbing way. The hunters were sitting on the ground, each with a bird in their lap, ripping out feathers one by one, until only a pink, wrinkly carcass was left – a meaty lump that seemed like it had never been a living thing at all. The hunters were a good distance away, but the wind was coming in our direction, and it brought the feathers with it. They landed on our food, blanket, clothes and even in our hair. Some of them were bloodstained.

"Nathan," Kate said at last. "Perhaps we should finish this back at the lighthouse."

Dad sighed. "All right. Sorry, gang. This was obviously a stupid idea."

"But Mummy!" Charlie wailed. "I don't want to go back to the lighthouse!"

"It'll be the same food," Kate said, trying to reassure him. "We'll just put it all on the kitchen table and—"

That was as far as she got before Charlie had

a meltdown. It was very piercing and annoying, so I kept my head down and helped shove the food back in the basket. A few minutes later, we were on our way, with Charlie keeping up a steady stream of complaints the whole time.

"I don't like the kitchen," he insisted. "It makes me feel weird. And there's someone under the table. They keep trying to grab my leg."

"Well, I'm sorry, Charlie, but the kitchen is where we're all going to be eating our meals for the next couple of weeks," Kate said, sounding exasperated. "So you'll just have to get used to it and stop making up silly stories."

Personally I didn't care where we ate as long as we ate somewhere. But when we got back to the lighthouse, Rosie cornered me before I could follow everyone inside.

"Look at this," she said, pressing her phone into my hands. "The lighthouse photo has come back."

I glanced down and saw that there was a blurry photo of the lighthouse set as her lock screen once again.

"You saw me delete it this morning, right?" Rosie went on. "But now it's back on my phone.

I noticed it just now when I turned it on. And that's not all."

She took the phone off me and tapped the screen a few times before holding it up. Her photo library didn't look right. Normally it was full of pictures, from selfies with her friends to gloomy landscape shots and arty photos of her food. But now it seemed that every single one of her photos was that same picture of the lighthouse, repeated hundreds of times.

Chapter Nine

"There must be something wrong with your phone," I said. "I mean, that's the only explanation."

"It's not the *only* explanation," Rosie replied.

I sighed. "You're not going to start on about the lighthouse being cursed, are you?"

"Don't you think it's a bit of a weird coincidence?" Rosie asked.

I was unsurprised to find that she looked excited rather than unsettled.

"I know you're a sceptic, Jess, but doesn't this prove that Will was right about the lighthouse? That it doesn't like being photographed?"

I shook my head. "Rosie, come on. That's just daft."

My sister rolled her eyes as she slipped the phone back into her pocket. "What's daft is you not believing the photographic evidence you're seeing with your own eyes."

Something about her tone suddenly made me suspicious, and I said, "How do I know this isn't your idea of a joke? It wouldn't be the first time you've played a trick on me with your photos. Remember that time you took a picture of my bedroom and then altered it to make it seem as if there was a ghost in the mirror?"

"I'm not playing a trick this time," Rosie replied.

"Well, that's what you insisted for months after that mirror photo," I said. "It took you ages to finally admit that it was a hoax."

"I *swear* that isn't happening this time."

She sounded genuine enough, but Rosie loved a bit of amateur dramatics, and I still didn't know whether to believe her or not.

"Well, if you're telling the truth, then it can't be long until you capture that award-winning ghost photo." I glanced through the kitchen window where I could see the food being laid out and said, "I'm going in to eat."

"Fine," Rosie said, still staring down at her phone. "I'll come in a minute."

I left her to it. In the kitchen, Dad and Kate were both fussing over Charlie, who was refusing to come out of the sitting room, so I took the opportunity to grab some food and take it upstairs. I didn't want to eat in our bedroom in case Rosie followed me there and started banging on about her phone again, but then I remembered the unlocked trapdoor leading up to the lighthouse tower. If I moved quickly, hopefully nobody would notice, and I could get some time to myself for half an hour.

It was easy to climb up the spiral staircase, slip through the trapdoor and close it behind me. Now that it was daytime, there was enough light coming in through the tower's small windows to see the staircase properly. It stretched up and up in a tight spiral like the inside of a shell. Staring at it made me feel slightly dizzy, so I looked at the steps beneath my feet instead and began to climb. I had to tread softly to avoid my shoes making loud *clang, clang, clang* noises on the metal stairs.

The curved granite walls looked bare at first, but then I saw the faint outline of fixtures and fittings that were no longer there, the ghostly silhouettes of old machinery once housed in the tower for some forgotten purpose. There was a great empty feeling about the place now, a hollowness that was almost heavy in the air.

I returned to the room where Will had been. Despite the creepy photos of the lighthouses on the wall, it was actually kind of nice to have a private space like this that no one else knew about. I sat behind the desk, opened a packet of crisps, and then my eyes fell on a logbook, still lying open.

12th November 1972

A fearsome storm ravaged Bird Rock yet again last night. The worst one yet. In fact, I haven't seen its like in more than twenty years. Was worried the shutters might blow away entirely, but upon inspection this morning the lighthouse appears mercifully undamaged — except for the damned eels that found their way into the pipes again. Savage brutes, they are — I once saw a conger eel bite clean through a length of chain down at the harbour. But they'll have to be fished out regardless.

Of more concern than the eels is the question of Hartley's state of mind. He seemed a

113

mild-mannered enough fellow when we first arrived, but now... Last night he swore he heard someone walking around in the Strangers' Room, and this morning he went outside and screamed at the gannets in the most unholy rage. I think he would have murdered every last one of those birds if he could. It was enough to make the blood run cold.

He appeared perfectly normal by the time we sat down to breakfast, but that only makes it worse in a way. These mood swings that come and go in the blink of an eye. Not at all a good temperament for a keeper. You want a calm, steady fellow beside you when working the lights.

1 a.m.

Why, now I begin to fear for my own sanity! Ferociously bad weather again this evening, so Hartley and I were going from room to room, making sure that all the shutters were secure, when I passed by the kitchen — a room I had myself only just checked — to see that the shutters on one of the windows had somehow opened. And then I saw a sight that made my blood run cold.

There were two small hands pressed up against the glass.

I froze to the spot, and for a long moment I could only stare at them. It wasn't Hartley out there for I could hear him calling down to me from the floor above. Besides, these hands were too small, the flesh too pale. Somehow, at some point, another person had arrived at Bird Rock. I strained my eyes for a face, a figure, but all I could see were those hands pressed against the glass, as if begging to be let in. I cannot explain why I felt such horror at the sight. They were only hands after all, yet there seemed something so terribly wrong about their whiteness compared with the dark night beyond. Something unnatural and awful.

Then they suddenly vanished and, with a start, I came back to myself. Someone was out there on Bird Rock, unprotected in the gale. They needed help, and ignoring Hartley's call, I threw on my waterproof and stepped out into the howling wind. Such a formidable gale! The rain lashed at my face as the wind tried to tear the coat from my back, and the salt seemed to fill up my lungs and make them ache. I struggled round to the kitchen window, half expecting to see a body slumped there, but there was nothing. No sign of any person at all. The sea was in a murderous mood, and I had no choice but to go back.

When I returned to the lighthouse and told Hartley what had happened, he insisted I must be seeing things. It does seem fantastical. And yet ... I did see hands at the window. I'm sure I did.

Sitting here now, alone on my watch, I start to wonder whether fear might be contagious. Perhaps I caught it from Hartley and the other men who served here before us. We all know the stories about Bird Rock. Nobody wants to be stationed here. Perhaps all that superstition has soaked into the stones of this old place and made it go strange and unnatural. Or maybe there has always been something strange and unnatural about the lighthouse itself, and that's why men dread it so. Then again, maybe it has merely been a long day and I am tired. The world will seem righter tomorrow.

John Porter

I leaned back in my chair, staring at the logbook, feeling an odd sense of dread creeping across my skin. I remembered that John Porter was the name of one of the last keepers ever to be stationed at Bird Rock. He was Cailean's grandfather, the one who had fallen to his death. It made my blood run cold that he had seen those hands too. And the mention of eels was unnerving, after what Rosie had said about her nightmare. But surely it was just a coincidence? People have nightmares, and my brother just happened to be outside playing and had decided to press his fingers against the glass, that's all. And yet ... the description of the hands was so familiar. The whiteness of them, the wrongness. That lighthouse keeper and I could have been looking at the exact same thing.

I carried on flicking through the logbooks for a little while and found multiple references to the Strangers' Room that Will had mentioned. As he'd said, it was located near the top of the tower, just below the lantern room itself, and seemed to be a sort of guest room for important visitors, including inspectors or poets, who came to write in peace. It was described as more ornate and comfortable than the other living areas, and the keepers were allowed to use the room when there were no guests on site, but they didn't seem to like it much. Several of them reported hearing strange noises from inside whenever it was unoccupied. And one of the keepers claimed he saw bloodstains appear on the floor…

I pushed the logbook away, shaking my head. These men had let their imaginations get the better of them, that was all. It was no surprise, given the setting. The island was so remote, and the flies and the birds would definitely become unbearable after a while.

I stood up, intending to go back downstairs, but then I noticed something about the lighthouse photos on the wall. They all had a single lit window. It was right at the top of the tower, where the Strangers' Room was supposed to be. Surely that hadn't been the case before, had it? My head buzzed with confusion. I couldn't know for certain, yet I felt sure that the lighthouses in the photos had all been dark a moment ago…

I rolled my eyes. Now *I* was the one letting my imagination run away. The windows must have been lit up all along. I stepped closer to the wall and felt a cold chill radiating from the old granite stones. It wasn't just the light in the photo that I hadn't noticed – there was also, quite clearly, a person standing at the window. Because the light was turned on behind, I couldn't make out a face – just a dark silhouette as they stared straight ahead. I recalled the lighthouse photo at the youth hostel back on the mainland, and the dark smudge that had seemed like a person. Now the figure wasn't only in one photo – it was in all of them.

There's someone in my room…

I leaned closer to the nearest photo, trying to make out some small detail of the face or clothes. My nose was only centimetres away…

When suddenly there was a thump and a shriek behind me.

Chapter Ten

I jerked round in time to see a white bird falling from sight and realized that a gannet must have flown into the window. I breathed a sigh of relief and turned back to pull the photo off the wall and examine the back. The words: Lighthouse at Bird Rock, Summer 1972 were written there in tidy handwriting. I glanced back up, and that's when I noticed that there was writing on the wall too, that had been hidden by the photo. Just two words written in block capitals in faded paint:

DON'T FORGET!

I frowned and reached for the other photos, pulling them down one by one until they fluttered to my feet in a heap. Every single one hid old painted messages on the wall behind. Just the same two words repeated over and over:

DON'T DON'T FORGET!
FORGET!
DON'T FORGET!

Forget what? Sometimes the words were tidy and uniform, but at others they looked like they'd been written by someone who was having difficulty holding the paintbrush or trying to use the opposite hand to the one they normally did, and then the letters wobbled and warped so badly that it was almost impossible to make them out.

Some of the words were written in such tiny letters that I had to squint to read them at all, but when I looked up at the ceiling, I noticed that someone had scrawled the words up there too in gigantic letters that took up the whole space and hurt my eyes to look at. The entire room suddenly seemed like it was shouting at me. I shivered as I recalled that some of the previous keepers were said to have lost their minds. Perhaps this was the handiwork of one of those tormented men.

I'd had more than enough of this weird place, so I slipped back down the spiral staircase and hurried to close the trapdoor. I didn't move quite fast enough, though. There were footsteps behind me and I turned to see Rosie emerging from our bedroom doorway.

"What's this?" she said, staring. "Did you find a way into the tower? I thought it was chained up."

I gestured at her to be quiet and then ushered her back into our bedroom. "Don't tell anyone," I said. "Will was here last night. He wanted to read the logbooks upstairs, so he cut the chain. Dad will be furious if he finds out."

I was worried that Rosie might ask *why* Will was so interested in the lighthouse. I certainly wasn't going to tell her the truth. Much as she loved ghost stories, she preferred them to be very old – like a missing keeper who'd disappeared a hundred years ago or a Victorian lady spotted beside a crumbling gravestone. Ever since her illness, she'd been especially sensitive to any real-life stories involving teenage girls dying before their time. Hearing about things like that could send her into a dark place for days and weeks on end sometimes. Fortunately she was too interested in the lighthouse itself to ask about Will's reasons for being there.

"And you weren't going to tell me?" she said, incredulous. "There must be the most amazing photo opportunities up there!"

She grabbed her camera from our room and then headed over to the spiral staircase. I knew it was useless trying to stop her – I'd seen that look on her face too many times before. She went straight up the stairs to the trapdoor, ignoring my hissed instruction to wait, and disappeared through it. My instinct was to follow, but I was worried that Dad might come looking for us, so I made myself hurry back downstairs to tell him that Rosie and I wanted some fresh air and were going for a walk. Luckily Dad and Kate were still preoccupied with how difficult Charlie was being, so they barely looked up to acknowledge what I'd said.

I left them to it and hurried back to the trapdoor, pulling it into place behind me before chasing after my sister. I hoped she might have started with the bottom rooms and that I'd find her fairly quickly, but there was no sign of her and I guessed she'd headed straight for the top of the tower. I gritted my teeth as I followed. With every step on the tightly wound spiral stairs, my knees became shakier and I could feel my palms growing sweaty as my vertigo kicked in.

There were fewer rooms than I had expected, and they felt more like chambers or prison cells than living spaces, with empty fireplaces that had all long-grown cold. Some of the walls and floors had faint imprints on them where furniture and machinery had once stood. I saw a row of fuel tanks with brass taps in one room, while another contained a living area. There were a couple of mouldy sofas, a coffee table and even a collection of chipped mugs on a dresser.

I'd thought the rooms would be empty and it was eerie seeing a living room set up like this, as if the former keepers might walk back in at any moment. A coil of rope and some old life jackets lay scattered on the floor, and a smell of saline damp and rusty metal hung about the place. There were dark brown blotches showing through the flaking paint.

I called out to Rosie a couple of times, but there was no answer and my voice seemed weirdly loud in such a confined space. I *really* didn't want to climb the tower any further. I thought about going back down and leaving Rosie to her ghost hunting, but that protective instinct had kicked in, and I knew I wouldn't be able to relax until I'd found her and made sure she was all right.

Trying to ignore my increasing vertigo, I forced myself to continue climbing until I was almost at the top of the tower. Here I finally found my sister, as well as what must surely be the Strangers' Room. Like Will had said, it was completely unlike any of the others. The furniture was long gone, but the room wasn't plain and simple; it was elaborately ornate with carved wooden panels on the walls, a mosaic floor and a domed ceiling. There was a large, curved mirror contained within a marble frame, topped with a model of a ship, and the fireplace was made from marble too. It felt all wrong for a lighthouse – too grand, like some kind of gilded bedchamber in a palace. A room that shouldn't have been there.

Rosie was standing by the fireplace and turned round to grin at me. "Isn't this *amazing*?" she said, gesturing at our surroundings. "Who'd ever expect to find something like this here?"

"I read about it in the logbooks," I said, stepping

inside. "They called it the Strangers' Room. It was meant to be a space for important visitors who were passing through, but the lighthouse keepers sometimes used it themselves too."

"Cool." Rosie beckoned me over, a look of excitement lighting up her face. "Check this out."

I joined her at the mantelpiece and saw that it wasn't bare like the others. A statuette of Jesus stood beside some sticks of incense, a crucifix and a small vial of water. It looked a bit like a shrine. Rosie picked up the little container of water, and I saw there was a label stuck to it proclaiming it to be holy water and bearing smudged ink writing.

Bird Rock Lighthouse
Consecrated on this date by
the Reverend George Drummond
PP (parish priest), 17.01.1973
In the presence of P. McCallister,
J. O. Wharton

It looked like there were a couple more names, but they were too blurry for me to read.

"I read about this online before we came," Rosie

said, beaming down at the little vial. "The last keepers thought the lighthouse was haunted so they had a priest come in."

She put the holy water back on the mantelpiece and raised her camera to snap a photo of it. The flash bounced off the glass of the mirror, which must have been made specially for the lighthouse. Where else would you find a curved looking glass? Like the one in the downstairs bathroom, this mirror was covered in old marks and a rusty patina that made it hard to see a reflection properly. Not only that but the curved shape of the glass distorted the image anyway, so that it was like looking into a mirror from a funfair attraction.

It made my head hurt and I turned away to glance out of the window instead, but then winced when I saw how toweringly high we were. To make it even worse, someone had scrawled a morbid piece of graffiti on the wall beside it. Just a single word, with an arrow pointing straight at the window:

JUMP!

I shuddered. Who would write such a thing?

Rosie said, "It's a bit gruesome, isn't it?"

"There's some weird graffiti in one of the rooms below too," I said. "Why don't you take a look at that?"

Rosie grinned. "You just don't want to be this high up."

"You're right, I don't."

"So go then. I'm quite happy here on my own. And I'm going to take loads of pictures, so I'll probably be here a while."

I sighed. The tower seemed safe enough – there were no gaping floorboards or crumbling walls, so I guessed it would be fine for Rosie to stay up here a bit longer.

"All right. If anyone asks where you are, I'll cover for you," I said. "Just don't spend hours up here, OK?"

I left her to it and made my way downstairs.

When Rosie joined me later that afternoon, she was buzzing with the photos she'd taken. I was only half paying attention when she showed me on her digital camera, but I saw that most of the pictures were of the Strangers' Room. I'd thought Rosie might spend a bit of time reading the logbooks, but when I said so she shook her head.

"I was going to but there's just something about this room." She stared down at the shot on her camera. "I don't know what it is yet... I'm going to go back up there tomorrow and take some photos with the Polaroid."

When we sat down for dinner later, and Dad asked about our walk, Rosie showed him some of the photos on her camera that she'd taken along the clifftop and the outside of the lighthouse the day before. It seemed our secret was safe for now, although of course we weren't the only ones who knew about the unlocked tower. I half thought that Will might sneak back once it got dark, but later that night a storm blew in from the sea, meaning that no one could reach the lighthouse. Or leave it.

Chapter Eleven

Days Three and Four

It rained non-stop for two entire days. Not only that but the wind was a gale that sounded like a beast trying to get inside the lighthouse. I could see why the keepers hadn't liked being stationed here during storms. It made everything seem even more claustrophobic and miserable when you couldn't go outside. I'd have given anything to be a hundred miles away from Bird Rock, back home, hanging out with my friends, but there was still more than a week to go on this horrible island.

The lighthouse felt crowded with all of us trapped inside, and the shutters rattled and banged so loudly that it became very difficult to sleep. Even when I did manage to doze, my dreams were strange, full of eels, birds and those pale hands. The power cut out several times, meaning we had to use candles. Lightning forked through the air.

Rosie couldn't get enough of the tower, but the last thing I wanted was to be up there in weather like this – it set off my vertigo too strongly. Which was why it especially annoyed me that I had to keep going up to drag Rosie out. She would disappear into the tower for hours, and I could only cover for her for so long. I could hardly say she'd gone for a walk with the storm raging outside.

To make it worse, she'd become more and more preoccupied with the Strangers' Room, which meant I had to climb almost to the top to fetch her. This happened on the first day of the storm and again on the second. I walked into the room, out of breath from the stairs, to find her just staring at her reflection in the curved mirror.

"Vain much?" I snapped. "You promised you'd only be half an hour this time, and it's been almost two. Don't tell me you've been staring at yourself in the mirror all this time?"

Rosie looked round at me, startled. "But I haven't," she said. "I haven't been here that long."

Thunder rumbled overhead, and the lights

flickered around us before plunging out. Luckily it was still the middle of the day, so it didn't go completely black, but the sky outside was so choked with clouds that the room became crowded with shadows.

"It's lunchtime," I said. "Dad told me to come and fetch you. We need to go back downstairs."

"But it can't be lunchtime," Rosie replied. "I've only been here a few minutes. Here, take a look at this." She held her camera out to me, and I saw a photo of the Strangers' Room displayed on the screen.

I took it from her impatiently. "What am I looking at?"

"Can't you see it?" Rosie whispered.

I glanced at her and was surprised that she looked oddly tense.

"I think there's a person." She leaned over me to point at the screen. "Right there. By the window."

I squinted back down at the photo. She must have taken it before she turned the lights on because the room was full of shadows, much as it was now. They created odd shapes on the walls and across the tiled floor. When I looked at the part of the room Rosie had pointed out, it seemed empty, so I shrugged

132

and said, "I don't know what you're talking about."

"There." Rosie jabbed at the screen again. "Right there. That's a shoulder. And that's the side of a head and part of a face. There's someone there, looking out of the window. But the room was empty when I took the picture."

I looked again, and now that she'd indicated the exact spot, the shadow seemed to morph before my eyes so that it *did* almost look like there might be a figure standing there, with its back to the camera…

I shook my head and returned her phone. "It's just a trick of the light," I said. "Plus it's barely noticeable. I don't think that photo is going to be the one to win you any ghost-hunting prizes. Perhaps you should keep looking for a lighthouse keeper's costume for Dad after all."

Rosie shrugged and a determined gleam suddenly came into her eye. "If I ever manage to photograph a ghost, I'd bet anything that it would be in this room. Hey, what do you think about having a sleepover up here? We could sneak up after everyone's gone to bed. Set the cameras running, see if they manage to capture anything—"

"Absolutely not."

She tried to argue with me, but I hustled her down the stairs so that we could have lunch.

I really hoped the weather cleared up before long. It was starting to feel like we did nothing except sit round the table. The island wasn't exactly pretty, but it would still be good to get out and have some fresh air. It didn't look as if that was going to happen any time soon, though. We'd barely sat down before lightning lit up the room. The thunder arrived seconds later, crashing so loudly that the windows rattled in their frames, and Charlie whimpered.

"It's a good thing the tower is locked," Kate said. "We wouldn't want to be up there in this weather. Lighthouses are often hit by lightning because of how tall they are."

I'd had no idea this was the case, but decided to make sure Rosie stayed away for the rest of the day. After lunch, I persuaded her to play a board game with Charlie and me. He'd been badgering us to join him all morning because the game required four players. I was surprised that he seemed to have gone weirdly quiet now and hardly spoke a word to either of us all through the game. He kept fiddling with a playing piece and glancing fearfully at the shuttered windows, flinching every time there was a new bolt of lightning. Everything about him seemed different from usual – smaller, and thinner, like he'd shrunk in on himself. A few seconds later, he rushed from the room without saying anything.

"Sorry, girls," Kate said, glancing over. "Please don't take it personally. I'm amazed he played a game with you at all. He's painfully shy right now."

She'd said that before but usually it seemed like Charlie was the opposite of shy. I'd certainly learned more snail facts over the last couple of days than I'd ever really wanted to know. And when I passed him on the stairs a short while later, he said, "Hi, Jess! Isn't the storm cool? It sounds like there's a monster trying to get in! *Roar!*"

I couldn't work him out at all, but then I really didn't know much about kids. Maybe sudden mood swings like this were common for a six-year-old?

I was heading to our bedroom when I noticed a piece of paper lying outside the door. I could see the bright flash of crayons and realized it was another one of Charlie's drawings. I bent to pick it up, thinking it would be more figures holding hands, but this was a different type of picture altogether.

Charlie had had to use a lot of red crayon because of all the blood splattered across the page.

There was a stick figure lying on the ground, or at least what was left of him. He seemed to be missing his legs, one of his hands and a chunk of his face. His mouth was a dark black scream of an O. All around were birds, swooping down at him with blood on their beaks and talons. I saw that one of them had an entire leg in its mouth, and another had a hand. They seemed to be eating him alive. I stared down at the drawing, wondering why Charlie would imagine something so grisly. I flipped the paper over to see if there was anything on the other side and, to my surprise, found lines of writing.

Dear Mama,

I hope you get this letter. It might be difficult to send because Papa says the birds have gone mad. He says they're ravenous, as if they haven't eaten in years and years, and that's making them do dreadful things. I know what it's like to be hungry, so I understand. Papa says the birds tried to eat the other lighthouse keeper. All of him — hair, skin, clothes and bones. If Papa hadn't been there, then there would have been nothing left of the other man. He was still hurt very badly, though. Papa says they've radioed for help, but the sea is too rough for anyone to come.

So we have to be careful and silent because the birds come into the lighthouse sometimes, and if you make any noise at all then they'll realize you're there and they'll find a way to get to you. They can only rip small pieces from you at a time so it would take ages to be eaten. Hours, probably, maybe days. But you can't fight them off because there are too many of them. Thousands and thousands on the island, Papa says. That's even more than a hundred.

Papa says it's fearsomely unnatural, and that God must be angry for some reason. I hope he stops being angry soon. I hope it isn't my fault. I'm sorry for all the bad things I've done. If I promise to be good from now on, perhaps I can come home?

Your loving son,

C

I stared down at the paper. Surely Charlie hadn't written this? The writing seemed too grown-up and neat for him. And I noticed now that the piece of paper was thick and crinkly and yellow, like it was old. I guessed Charlie must have found the letter somewhere and used the back of it for his drawing.

My mind went to the logbooks and documents upstairs in the tower. I was just wondering whether Charlie could have found his way up there when the trapdoor suddenly shifted to one side and down climbed Charlie himself. He started guiltily when he saw me and darted into his bedroom, but I followed him and closed the door behind us.

"Charlie, you shouldn't have been up there," I said. "What were you thinking?"

"We were only playing," he replied, sticking out his lower lip.

"We?" I repeated. "Who's 'we'?"

"Me and my friend. We were exploring the tower."

I guessed he must have some kind of imaginary friend, which was confirmed the next moment when Charlie said, "No one else can see him."

"Well, both of you keep out of the tower from now on. You heard what your mum said about the lightning strikes. It's not safe."

"OK," Charlie said cheerfully enough. "It's boring up there anyway."

He scampered off and I stood for a moment, worrying about what to do. Maybe I should tell Dad and we could find some way of locking the door again. But when I suggested as much to Rosie later that day, she was crestfallen and begged me not to.

"I'm getting the most fantastic photos!" she exclaimed. "And if I carry on then I just know I'll capture something supernatural on film before we leave. I can *feel* it!"

Even though I knew it was a bad idea, I gave in to Rosie, just like I always did. So I agreed to leave the trapdoor open and keep it a secret from Dad and Kate.

It wasn't until much later that I'd realize this was the biggest mistake of my life.

That night Rosie was still extremely keen on the idea of sleeping in the Strangers' Room, but the storm was raging worse than ever so I told her it was absolutely not an option. In the end she reluctantly agreed to set up her digital camera on video-recording mode in the room and collect it the next morning.

We lay down to sleep in utter darkness as usual. I would never have admitted it to Rosie, but I found the complete lack of light a bit unnerving. At home, I was used to street lamps shining through the curtains, and it still seemed unnatural for it to be so pitch-black, with nothing to help my eyes adjust to the dark at all. I almost envied Charlie his night light.

After a while I fell into a weird dream where Rosie was taking photos of me in the Strangers' Room. Her camera flashed against the warped glass of the mirror, but for some reason the pictures seemed to make her very upset.

"You're not in them!" she kept saying, a wild look in her eye as she thrust the Polaroids at me. "I'm pointing the camera right at you, but you're not there! You're not there!"

I looked down and saw that she was right. The photos in my hands showed only one girl in the room, and that was Rosie. The photos didn't capture me or my reflection in the mirror. It was only my sister there alone, looking more and more panic-stricken.

"This isn't right!" she said. "Let me try again!"

She raised the camera, and the flash went off in my face, making my eyes smart, and I blinked.

"That's enough," I protested. "You're blinding me with that thing!"

But she ignored me, and there was only the whir, click, flash until she finally lowered the camera and I saw that it wasn't Rosie holding the camera at all – it was me. My head whirled with confusion as I realized that Rosie had vanished. When had that happened? How had we swapped places, and how had I missed it?

The camera in my hands was still going off, even though I wasn't pressing any buttons. The sound of the shutter coming down seemed to get louder and louder until finally the Strangers' Room melted away and I jerked upright in my sleeping bag in the bedroom I was sharing with Rosie. A dream. That was all it was. Just a dream. And yet … there was still a camera going off somewhere. I could hear it. The first click and flash disoriented me, but when it came a second time I realized it was coming from the corner of the room.

"Rosie, what the hell?" I said. "Cut it out."

Taking photos of me while I was asleep was a whole new level of weird, even for my sister. But then the camera went off a third time and – in the brief moments that the flash lit up the room – I saw, quite clearly, that Rosie was lying sound asleep beside me.

Chapter Twelve

Day Five

"Rosie!" My hand flew out, and I shook her roughly. "Wake up!"

"What?" I felt her sit up beside me. "What's happening?"

"There's someone in here with us."

I thrashed around in my sleeping bag, desperate to get out so I could turn the light on, but the zip seemed to be stuck. Meanwhile the camera went off again and again.

Click, flash!

Click, flash!

Click, flash!

"Who's there?" Rosie cried out, and I could hear the fear in her voice.

Whoever was holding the camera didn't say

a word, but I could tell they were coming closer towards us because the floorboards groaned beneath their feet, and every time the flash went off it seemed bigger and brighter. The next time the room lit up for a second, I kept my eyes open wide, trying to make out who was there, but the flash was too dazzling and made everything jerk and dance around us. I could hear Rosie's breath coming in panicked gasps as she grabbed tightly on to my arm. My hand flailed around for my phone but I only managed to send it sliding along the floor away from me.

Click, flash!

"Charlie, is that you?" I said into the darkness. "It's not funny. Stop it."

Finally I found Rosie's phone and swiped to bring up the torch. At the same moment, there was a loud thump as the camera fell to the floor. The torch beam sliced through the room, illuminating the camera lying a few paces away. I swept the light across the room, making the shadows jump around us. Our door was open but there was nobody in the room except me and Rosie.

"It must have been Charlie," I said, my voice

shaking slightly with adrenaline. "I guess that was his idea of a joke."

Rosie was staring at her camera. "But … I didn't hear him run out. And that's the camera I left running in the Strangers' Room," she said.

"Charlie's been playing up in the tower," I replied, finally managing to yank the zip of my sleeping bag free. "He must have taken the camera, even though he *promised* me he wouldn't go up there again."

I stormed into the corridor and – sure enough – Charlie was just coming out of the bathroom. I told him off about what had just happened – maybe a little more crossly than I should have – but predictably he denied everything. It *must* have been him, though, since it obviously wasn't Dad or Kate.

When I went back to our room, Rosie was flicking through the photos on the camera and I got a brief glimpse of the two of us sitting up in our sleeping bags, looking terrified.

"Could you just delete those?"

"I am," Rosie replied. "But Jess, look. I went back through the footage from the Strangers' Room. It was recording up there for an hour before someone switched it off."

She held it up but the screen just showed an empty room.

"So what?" I asked impatiently.

"Can't you see it?" she replied. "There's something there. In the mirror."

"Probably Charlie's reflection as he steals the camera," I said. "Look, would you put that thing away? I'm tired and I'd like to get *some* sleep tonight."

Rosie reluctantly put the camera to one side. I was a bit surprised she didn't seem more pleased by whatever it was she thought she'd captured on screen. It was as if it had suddenly stopped being a game to her and had become something real instead.

The next morning she kept on about the photos, poring over the footage on her camera and thrusting it into my face until I got sick of her pointing out tiny shadows and smudges on the screen, convinced there was something there.

"Maybe we should ask that guga hunter, Will, about it?" Rosie finally suggested. "He might be able to tell us more about the Strangers' Room?"

I shook my head. I still hadn't said anything to

Rosie about Will's sister dying, and I didn't want Will to mention it either. "I think you should just do what Dad asked and stay away from him," I said. "He's unfriendly and rude."

Rosie didn't say anything more about it, and I hoped that was an end to the conversation. The storm had finally blown over and it was such a relief to see some blue sky and sunshine again. After two days of being cooped up inside it, I'd grown sick of the lighthouse, so I was happy to spend a bit of time outside in the keeper's garden with Charlie, even when we were just poking around in the dirt, looking for snails. He still refused to admit that he'd been the one in our bedroom with the camera, but I guessed he just didn't want to get into trouble over it. I thought about mentioning it to Dad, but then I'd risk him finding out about the trapdoor, and besides, it seemed mean to tell tales on Charlie. Also, after two days of being locked up together, I just wanted to get away from Dad and Kate for a bit too.

When I went upstairs to fetch Rosie for lunch a couple of hours later, she wasn't there. I knew she was probably back in the Strangers' Room, and sure enough when I climbed the spiral staircase, I found her. Or rather I found her rushing from the room so quickly that she almost ran straight into me.

"Hey, watch it!" I exclaimed. "You almost sent us both down the stairs." Then I saw her ashen face and said, "What's the matter?"

She swallowed hard, cast a wary look back into the room and said, "There's... I think there's something wrong with the mirror in there."

I looked over her shoulder at the old mirror on the wall. "You mean that it's concave?" I said. "Or covered in rust? Either way, it's quite hard to see anything clearly in it."

"No, no, it's something more than that. It's... You know that thing where you stare in the mirror for so long that you almost don't recognize yourself any more? Well, something similar just happened to me, but it wasn't only that. It was... For a second, I actually... I couldn't remember who I was."

I rolled my eyes. "Sounds like you're spending too much time cooped up inside. Look, the sun is finally shining. Why don't you go for a walk along the cliffs after lunch? Take photos of the birds or something."

I was pleased when Rosie agreed to my suggestion and went out after lunch. I would have liked to get out of the lighthouse for a bit and go with her, but I was afraid she'd just bang on about haunted mirrors, so I got some music up on my phone and soaked up the sun in the garden instead. It was kind of nice to begin with. Then as the time passed by and Rosie didn't come back, I started to worry. I'd only expected her to be gone half an hour or so, but soon a couple of hours had passed and she was still out.

It was impossible to know which part of the island she was on, and I didn't want to walk round in circles for hours, so I gritted my teeth and climbed the spiral staircase back to the Strangers' Room, thinking that I might be able to spot her from the window. When I walked in, my eyes were drawn to that horrible piece of graffiti, the single word:

JUMP!

There was something eerily persuasive about it, as if it wasn't merely a painted word but a voice whispering in my ear, or inside my mind, daring me to do it... I shook my head and looked out of the window. I saw Rosie at once. It would have been impossible to spot her from the lower windows, but I had a good view over much of the island from this height, and there she was, a little way along the cliff path. To my dismay, she wasn't alone. Will was with her. They stood close together, their heads bent over something, and I guessed Rosie was showing him the photos and video on her camera.

But then, all of a sudden, Rosie recoiled with a sudden jerky movement that almost sent her tumbling to the ground. She looked up at Will just once, and then she was running away from him like her life depended on it, back along the path towards the lighthouse. Will didn't make any attempt to follow her, and I saw that the object in his hands wasn't a camera, but a phone. He slipped it into his pocket and slowly looked up at the lighthouse.

I couldn't make out his expression properly from this distance and didn't think there was much chance he'd be able to spot me, but I found myself stepping back instinctively. The heel of my shoe came down on something that felt like a foot, as if there was someone standing directly behind me, but when I turned round there was no one there. There had to be an explanation – I'd probably just trodden on a loose tile or something … but it had *really* felt as if there was a person there, and suddenly I really didn't want to be in the Strangers' Room any more. I didn't want to be in the room at all.

I left as quickly as I could, my heart beating uncomfortably fast in my chest. I had no idea what Will had said to Rosie, but he'd obviously upset her, so it was probably something about his sister. I hurried out of the tower and went along the cliff path to meet her. There were tears pouring down her face when she rounded the corner and almost ran straight into me. I had to grab on to her arm to force her to stop.

"Hey, what's going on?" I said. "What's wrong?"

"We have to leave the lighthouse," she gasped, her hands trembling as she pushed her hair out of her face. "Someone died there, a girl my age, just last summer. I saw it! That guga hunter, Will, he showed me a video of it happening on his phone."

"He did *what?*" I stared at her, feeling a bit sick.

I'd been worried that Will might mention his sister, but it had never occurred to me that he would have a video of her death on his phone, let alone that he

150

would show it to Rosie.

"She died!" Rosie went on. "There was so much blood, and her head, it … it was all over the ground!" She began to cry again, tears pouring down her face.

"Oh, Rosie." I was so furious with Will that I could hardly get the words out. "I don't know what the hell he was thinking, showing you a video like that, but even if there was an accident here last year it doesn't mean that—"

She shook her head and was already backing away. "No, you don't understand. The lighthouse is haunted. I mean *really* haunted. I can't stay here, Jess, I can't!"

I tried to reach for her but she'd already pushed past me and was running back down the cliff path, probably to tell Dad what she'd just told me. My hands bunched into fists and I cursed Will under my breath. I should have told Dad what he was up to sooner. As soon as I got back, I would explain about the bolt cutters and the trapdoor. We would lock everything up tight again, and if I saw Will anywhere near the lighthouse then I wouldn't hesitate to raise the alarm. But I had a few things I wanted to say to him first, so I marched along the path to the hunters' camp.

When I got there, I spotted Will's lone figure striding towards one of the stone bothies. Ignoring the curious glances of the other hunters, I went straight after him, not caring who saw or heard us.

"Hey!" I grabbed hold of his arm, forcing him to turn round. "How dare you frighten my sister like that? She's crying her eyes out because of you!"

He shook me off. "Frighten her?" he exclaimed in a frustrated voice. "I'm trying to save her life! I'm trying to save you. She should be frightened. You should *all* be frightened."

"Just tell me you didn't *really* show her a video on your phone of your sister dying?" I said. "Surely no one could be that messed up?"

Part of me was still hoping this might all be some kind of misunderstanding, but Will only shrugged and said, "Better for her to see it happen to someone else than to have it happen to her—"

My anger bubbled right over, and I found myself shoving Will hard in the chest with both hands. "You're *sick!*" I shouted, my voice tearing slightly with the rage I couldn't contain. "You're so wrapped up in your own drama but you have no idea what my sister's been through or what a video like that

152

could do to her! Just stay the hell away from her – from all of us!"

The yelling had drawn the other hunters to us, including Will's father, who I recognized from the hostel. I felt Cailean's hand on my arm, pulling me back, just as my dad arrived at the camp. I was surprised to see him as normally he hated confrontation of any kind, but there he was beside me, thrusting Cailean away and grabbing my hand.

"Don't touch my daughter!" he snapped.

Cailean immediately raised his hands in an appeasing gesture. "I'm only trying to diffuse the situation," he said calmly. "That's all. Perhaps someone might like to tell me exactly what's going on?"

Dad repeated what Rosie had told me – that Will had shown her a video on his phone of his sister dying at the lighthouse.

The colour drained from Will's father's face. He closed his eyes briefly. "Please, Will," he said, so quietly that I almost didn't hear him. "Please tell me that video isn't still on your phone. I *saw* you delete it."

"I deleted it because you forced me to," Will

replied. "But I'd already made copies and—"

His dad moved so fast that no one had a chance to stop him, grabbing Will by the front of his jacket and shoving him up so hard against the wall of the bothy that the back of his head struck against the stone with a horrible crack.

"You sick bastard!" he shouted. "Delete it! Now! Then you'll apologize to this man and his daughter."

"No," Will said. His voice came out in a gasp, but there was a hard glint in his eye. "Someone has to warn them about the lighthouse. It killed Kenzie, and now it might—"

"That lighthouse didn't kill your sister," Will's dad shouted. "You did!"

There was an awful silence. A look of horror crossed Will's father's face the moment he spoke, and I could tell that he regretted his words, but it was too late to take them back. He let go of Will and stumbled away from him. Then he took a deep, steadying breath. "Will. I didn't mean—"

"Yes, you did," Will said in a flat tone. "And it's fine; you're right. It is my fault. It's about time someone finally had the guts to say it out loud, to my face."

"Look, you clearly have your own ... issues going on," my dad said. He looked massively uncomfortable, as if he wanted to be anywhere other than here. "Just stay away from my family."

"I'm really sorry about the boy," Will's dad said. "It's no excuse but he hasn't been right since his sister passed away. It won't happen again."

Dad gave a stiff nod. "Come on, Jess."

He gripped my arm and I had no choice but to follow him back down the path. As soon as we were out of earshot, he started lecturing me about the fact that I'd gone to the hunters' camp by myself, and this lasted pretty much all the way back to the lighthouse, where we found Rosie still crying in the kitchen, with Kate desperately trying to comfort her.

"Did you see the video?" she asked, looking up at us with a tear-stained face.

"No, of course not," Dad replied. He kneeled in front of her. "Sweetheart, it's really appalling that he showed you something like that. I'm so sorry. I hope you can try to put it behind you, and we can still have a nice summer together, but if you really feel you can't forget what you saw and that you don't want to stay here any more then I understand and

I'll radio for a boat to come and fetch you, all right? But please, let's just sleep on it. It's too late to get a boat here today anyway. Let's just get a good night's rest, and if you still feel this way tomorrow then I'll call for a boat first thing in the morning."

A look of relief washed over Rosie's face. "You'll come too, won't you, Jess?"

"Of course," I replied, squeezing her hand. "Anywhere you go, I go too. You know that."

"You might feel better about things tomorrow," Dad said, a little pleadingly.

"I won't," Rosie said forcefully. "I'll stay here tonight if I have to, but tomorrow I want to leave as soon as I can." She gave a little shudder. "And I don't ever want to come back to Bird Rock again."

That evening Rosie packed up all her stuff so she'd be ready to go in the morning. It seemed she was determined that we'd both be leaving Bird Rock as soon as possible, and I was more than happy to go along with her. It was a boring, gross, horrible place with nothing to do. And ... for those few moments back in the Strangers' Room it really *had* felt as if there was someone in there with me. I didn't know what was going on in this weird place, and I didn't care. I was just keen to get off the island as quickly as possible.

"I left some of my crystals on the mantelpiece in the Strangers' Room," Rosie said. "I'll just go and fetch them."

"OK. And when you're back we need to tell Dad about the trapdoor so he can lock it again. I don't think Charlie should be playing up there on his own."

Rosie went off and I started to pack my own bag. She still hadn't come back by the time I finished, and in the end I decided to go and look for her. As soon as I stepped out of our bedroom, I spotted another one of Charlie's drawings on the floor outside our room. I bent to pick it up and a shiver ran over me. He'd drawn a stick-figure girl in the Strangers' Room, looking into the mirror there.

I could tell it was meant to be the Strangers' Room because the mirror was curved and had a large frame, with a ship perched on top of it. He'd also drawn the window behind her, complete with the word **JUMP!** Seeing it inside a child's drawing made me shiver, but worse than that was the girl herself. In the room, she had a smile on her face, but her reflection had a big frown, and there was something weird and chilling about the difference. I flipped the drawing over to see if there was another letter there, and sure enough the same neat writing was printed along the back.

Dear Mama,

It has been several days but Papa says that the birds are still dangerous and savage. They've been attacking the keepers whenever they step outside the lighthouse, diving at them really fast, faster than you would believe unless you saw it for yourself. Their beaks are sharp and they can rip a chunk of hair straight from your head or tear a long strip of flesh off your face. The birds have a bloodlust, Papa said, and it's a nasty one. Bloodlust means they want to hurt things.

And Papa says he finally knows what's causing it. It's not an illness like we first thought — it's the lighthouse. The birds that get inside the building go mad. Papa found a whole load of them in the Strangers' Room the other day, and he said they were all just standing on the floor, staring up into the mirror, and they must have been there for hours. It was like they'd been staring into the mirror for so long that they'd forgotten they were birds at all...

Papa says it's unnatural and unholy, a judgement from God. I pray every night that it will get better soon, and I will see you again. It's so lonely here. Even more than the workhouse.

Your loving son,

C

I frowned at the letter, remembering Rosie's words from before: *You know that thing where you stare in the mirror for so long that you almost don't recognize yourself any more? Well, something similar just happened to me… For a second, I actually… I couldn't remember who I was.*

I climbed the spiral staircase after her. When I got to the Strangers' Room, there was no sign of Rosie, but the window was open and I saw a single gannet perched on the windowsill, cocking its head this way and that, staring at me with beady eyes. I felt a strong tug of unease, both about the bird and the window. I'd never seen it open before, and something about this felt wrong. The word **JUMP!** suddenly seemed clearer and darker, as if the letters had been burned into the wall rather than merely painted there.

This close, the gannet seemed massive, and my

mind went to those weird letters I'd found on the back of Charlie's drawings. You'd definitely have a problem if a bird this size decided to attack you. Its beak and claws looked horribly sharp, and I had to force myself to walk over and wave it away.

"Go on, shoo!"

To my relief, it fluttered off with a squawk, and I reached out for the window, my fingers shaking at the awful proximity to the sickening height. I couldn't help my eyes sliding downwards, and my heart suddenly seemed to stop inside my chest. I couldn't breathe, or think, or do anything other than stare in horror at the bent and crooked shape of a body, just visible in the moonlight, crumpled upon the ground, right at the foot of the lighthouse.

Chapter Thirteen

A cloud shifted in the sky above, the moonlight became a little brighter, and suddenly there was no body on the ground at all – only a shadow breaking up before my eyes, an illusion caused by the night. My heart began beating again, but now it felt like it was going at about a hundred beats a second, and my hands shook worse than ever as I slammed the window closed. I knew Rosie must be in the lighthouse somewhere – that I had gone in the wrong direction and missed her – yet I suddenly had the most awful, awful feeling. Something was wrong – I knew it.

I strode over to the mantelpiece and saw that Rosie's crystals were still there, so I scooped them up and slipped them into my pocket. If Rosie hadn't come up here to fetch the crystals, then where had she gone? I thought perhaps she might be in one of the other rooms inside the tower and was just about to check when something caught my eye in the curved mirror. I turned towards it and then breathed a sigh of relief. Rosie was here after all – I could see her in the reflection, standing with her back to me, peering out of the window I'd just closed. I guessed she must have entered the room behind me, moving so quietly that I hadn't heard her come in.

"Where have you been?" I began. "I was—"

I turned round and broke off abruptly, the words dying in my throat. The room was empty. Rosie wasn't there. There was no one in front of the window. My eyes went back to the mirror and it now showed only me in the room. But how could that be? Rosie had been right there – she couldn't possibly have walked, or even run from my sight in the split second it had taken me to turn round. My head whirled and throbbed with confusion. What was going on?

"Rosie?" I called, even though I could see she wasn't there.

With a last glance around, I hurried out on to the

spiral staircase and looked up at the lantern room. I'd never been brave enough to go up there before, but now I ran quickly up the staircase, right to the top. I was suddenly very glad it was dark because this room had gigantic, triple-height, plate-glass windows. There were a couple of large, circular mirrors lying on the floor, and a huge, three-and-a-half-metre optic dominated the centre of the room, pulsing out a blindingly bright light at intervals. A metal gantry ran round the walls above — I guessed so that keepers and maintenance crew could reach the lantern. But there was no sign of Rosie anywhere.

I made my way back down the tower, checking each room and calling her name as I went. Finally I slipped out through the trapdoor and ran downstairs to where Dad, Kate and Charlie were playing cards at the kitchen table.

"Do you know where Rosie is?" I asked. "I can't find her."

"I haven't seen her," Dad replied. "Did she go outside for some air?"

I looked out of the window. For a moment, I thought I saw the imprint of white hands pressed against the glass, but then I blinked and there was nothing but fog. A wave of dizziness hit me and I clenched my hands together tightly. What the hell was going on?

"It's really foggy outside," Kate said. "She shouldn't be out in this – she might lose sight of the path. Hey, are you OK? You look a bit pale."

"I'm fine. I'm just worried about Rosie."

Dad and Kate both got up and said they'd help me look for her.

"Can I come too?" Charlie asked.

"No, wait here," Kate told him. "We'll be right back."

I hurried to the front door, and when I stepped outside the fog was like a blanket that immediately wrapped itself around me, making it hard to breathe.

"Rosie?" I called.

There was nothing but silence. Even the birds and the flies were quiet. I realized I couldn't even hear the sea. The fog had smothered everything.

"Rosie!" I called again.

"I'm sure she's just round the corner," Dad said from beside me. "Why don't you go back inside, and Kate and I will find her?"

I shook Dad off, switched on my phone's torch and began to walk round the lighthouse. "You two go the other way," I called over my shoulder. "Then we won't miss her."

The weak beam from the torch didn't help much with the fog, and I couldn't see any sign of Rosie. When I got about halfway round, I expected to run into Dad and Kate coming from the other direction, but – to my surprise – they never appeared. Soon enough, I was right back where I'd started, beside the front door.

"Rosie!" I called again.

There was no response, nothing. Awful images filled my head of Rosie falling from a cliff edge into the dark sea. I tried to control my rising panic and think. My sister wasn't stupid – she wouldn't have gone wandering off in the fog, no matter how upset she was. Yet I was certain she was no longer inside the lighthouse either. Something had *happened* to her. I knew it.

My T-shirt was damp with sweat, and I was gasping, struggling to breathe in the fog. I couldn't just go back inside and wait for the weather to clear. I had to find Rosie. So I set off away from the lighthouse. Surely if I went very slowly, carefully feeling my way and not straying from the path, then it would be all right.

I knew Dad would forbid it, so I didn't bother to go and find him first. I just left, inching my way along, calling out Rosie's name. By the light of my torch, I could see the tiny bit of path directly in front of me, but that was all. The fog felt like cold fingers stroking my skin, and I shivered. The taste of the sea had never been so strong on my lips, and it was no longer only salt but also seaweed, spiny fish and the skeletal ribs of forgotten underwater wrecks.

A gannet was startled into sudden flight somewhere to my right, and I yelped at the sound of beating wings. I felt the sleek softness of feathers brush against my face. But I still couldn't see anything except for the area directly in front of me. A chilly breeze tugged at my clothes and I felt as if it wanted to drag me right over the edge of the cliff.

I continued to inch my way along the path when suddenly, out of nowhere, I heard humming – a woman's voice, ghostly and sorrowful. I stopped in shock, but then the sound melted away and it didn't feel real. The hairs on my arms stood up, and I told myself it must have been the echo of the waves crashing in the unseen caves below.

Time seemed to unravel in the fog and it was hard to tell how long I'd been out there. Was it five minutes or an hour? Maybe this was a dream? Maybe I'd wake up any minute now, tucked up beside Rosie in our sleeping bags... But the fog was too cold and wet on my skin, and I knew I was awake, that this was really happening. I carried on searching and yelling Rosie's name until I was hoarse.

Finally I stopped on the path, exhausted. I hoped that Dad and Kate were out doing the same thing over on the other side of the island. Maybe they'd already found Rosie, and she was safely back with them? Perhaps I should go back to the lighthouse now and make sure? The thought of returning without my sister was awful, but she *could* already be there. And I was getting thoroughly sick of the fog and the quiet, and the sense that there were hundreds of shiny bird eyes looking at me silently from the darkness. In the end I decided to check the lighthouse. If she wasn't there, then I'd come straight out again.

Only ... somehow ... I'd got lost. The fog had lifted enough for me to see a metre or so in front of me, but the path curled in the opposite direction to what I'd been expecting. And although I followed it for quite a long way, there was no sign of the lighthouse, which surely should have appeared by now. How had I managed to get turned around?

I continued to follow the path, not knowing what else to do, when – suddenly – a figure appeared up ahead. He was facing away from me, and I thought it was Dad, but then I realized this man was wearing a dark woollen coat that reached to his knees, along with a stiff-peaked cap. Dad didn't own anything like that. It looked like a uniform. Perhaps the kind a lighthouse keeper might wear… For a wild moment, I wondered whether Rosie had found the outfit in one of the lighthouse cupboards and persuaded Dad to dress up in it to give me a scare. Perhaps this was just an elaborate prank, and Dad and Kate were in on it too…

But the man before me was shorter and stockier than Dad. He stood completely still, all alone in the middle of the fog, staring out at nothing with his hands loose by his sides. I tried to tell myself that he might be one of the guga hunters, yet I knew somehow that he wasn't. All of a sudden, I *really* didn't want him to turn round and see me.

My breath came in shallow gasps as I staggered back the way I'd come, only to find that there was another person on the path up ahead. A woman this time, dressed in a long, old-fashioned white nightdress, with dark hair that reached to the small of her back. She was barefoot, absolutely motionless, and stood facing away from me. She could almost have been a statue if it wasn't for the breeze stirring her nightdress and hair. I felt the same sense of wrongness pouring off her that I had from the man. Was she a ghost? Was that why the sight of her felt so strange?

Suddenly I was angry with myself, and my hand tightened around my phone. I must be losing my mind. There was no such thing as ghosts. If there was someone on the path up ahead of me, then they were real, and perhaps they'd seen Rosie and could point me in her direction. There must be a woman in the guga hunters' party – perhaps I was near their camp?

"Hello?" I called, taking a step closer.

The woman didn't turn round, didn't acknowledge having heard me at all, yet there was no way she could have failed to do so.

"I'm lost," I tried, walking closer. "Can you tell me

the way to the lighthouse?"

At the word *lighthouse*, the woman stiffened, but still she didn't move. I could feel anger and fear mixing together in my stomach as I finally reached her.

"Hey!" I said. "Didn't you hear—?"

She spun round and I leaped back, longing to scream, but my throat had closed up and I couldn't make a single sound. The woman had no face, just a mass of sharp, pointed beaks where it should have been. As I stared, sickened, the beaks exploded and the woman seemed to break apart in a swarm of screeching gannets, all swooping and diving at me as if determined to run me right off the island.

I fled. The birds followed me in a flurry of beating wings for a few moments before scattering. I no longer cared about the fog or the cliff edge, and thoughts of finding Rosie vanished for the moment too – all I cared about was getting back to the shelter of the lighthouse. I ran and ran without finding it, but I saw more people around me in the fog. There was a tall, slim man wearing the same uniform as the first figure and an ancient-looking man in a waterproof coat. There was even a little boy and girl wearing old-fashioned clothes and holding hands.

They all stood completely motionless, staring straight ahead with their backs to me. I couldn't seem to avoid them. When I changed direction, another loomed up in my path, and I could just make out the silhouettes of others further away as well. Sobbing, I spun round yet again and staggered through a clearing, only to crash straight into someone. I went sprawling backwards, landed on the ground with a grunt, and instinctively raised my hands to my face, not wanting to see any more beaks bursting through people's faces.

But then a voice I recognized said, "Jess?"

I looked up to see Will staring down at me, an expression of shock on his face. And beyond him were flickering campfires and the hunched stone silhouettes of the ancient black houses.

I had found the guga hunters' camp.

Chapter Fourteen

A sob of relief burst from my throat as Will reached out a hand and hauled me to my feet.

"Thank you!" I gasped. "I thought… Oh God, I thought—"

"You thought you would die, and you almost did!" Will exclaimed. "Why are you even out on a night like this? Can't you see it's not safe?"

"My sister!" I gasped. "She's missing, and I have to find her!"

The other hunters had noticed me by then and hurried over, all wearing concerned expressions.

"There are people!" I gasped. "Out there in the fog! I saw them!"

Then the fear and the panic got the better of me, and I burst into tears.

"For Chrissake, lassie!" Cailean exclaimed. "You can't be wandering around at night in this weather. You'll dive straight off the edge of the cliff! What were you thinking of?"

When I tried to tell them about the people in the fog, they all insisted there was no one else on Bird Rock.

"What about my sister?" I asked, wiping my eyes on my sleeve and trying to pull myself together. "Have you seen her?"

The hunters were already shaking their heads. "We haven't seen anyone," one of them replied. "If you've got any sense, then you stay put when the fog comes."

I shivered. "I have to get back to the lighthouse."

"You're not going anywhere right now, missy," Cailean said firmly. "I won't have your death on my conscience." He patted my arm and his voice was gentle. "Look, it's easy to see shapes in the fog. Easy to get turned round and confused. Why, I bet it was the cairns you saw! Damn eerie they look in the moonlight too. There's not one of us here who hasn't been spooked by them at one point or another. Isn't that right?"

He looked to the other hunters for support, and they nodded in agreement – all except Will, who stood with his arms folded, watching me closely.

I groaned aloud. "I know the difference between a person and a *cairn*!"

"Soon as the fog clears, someone will take you back to the lighthouse," Cailean said. "In the meantime, you might as well sit down and have a cup of tea."

I tried to argue but Cailean absolutely refused to budge. When I made to walk away, he gripped my arm gently but firmly. "Soon as the fog lifts," he said. "And not a moment before."

It seemed I had no choice. Part of me was glad because the thought of going back into the fog alone and coming across those strange, silent people filled me with the most unspeakable dread, so I let them steer me to a seat beside the fire and accepted a hot mug of tea. It *did* taste good, and my hands gradually stopped shaking as I held it.

I so badly wanted to believe that I had imagined those ghostly figures, like the hunters said, but I knew I hadn't. Whoever and whatever they were, they had been there. Once they seemed sure I wasn't going to run away, the hunters gave me a little space, although they never moved too far. Before long, Will came and sat down by my side.

"I believe you," he said quietly. "About the people in the fog."

I felt a flicker of hope. "Have you seen them too?"

"No. But nothing would surprise me on Bird Rock. I told you strange things would happen if you stayed at the lighthouse. Your family woke it up when you started living there."

I stared at him. "What do you mean, we *woke* it up?" I asked, struggling not to crumple beneath a wave of despair. "It's a building. It's not aware of us one way or another. It's not *alive*."

"Don't be so sure about that," Will replied. "Don't be sure about anything on Bird Rock. I still haven't figured out whether it's the lighthouse, or a presence inside it, but there's *something* sentient there. Something that watches, and feels things, and hates us for being here. Something that wants us all to go away."

"Maybe you're right," I replied. "Something really messed up is going on here. You tried so many times to warn us. I should have listened, and I'm sorry. Sorry for yelling at you earlier, and for getting you into trouble with your dad, and—"

Will took my hand with surprising gentleness, his fingers warm and reassuring around mine. "Forget it. I knew that sharing that video would seem monstrous. It *was* monstrous – a cruel thing to do." A muscle twitched in his jaw. "I hated myself for it but I couldn't think what else to do to persuade you to leave."

"We'll go," I said. "As soon as I find my sister, we'll make my dad see that we *all* need to leave Bird Rock. We're not staying here another night."

Will nodded and gave my hand a quick squeeze before releasing it. "Good," he said, breathing a sigh of relief. "That's good. Hopefully it's all just a misunderstanding with your sister, and she's already back at the lighthouse."

I hoped so with all my soul, but I had a terrible feeling in the pit of my stomach. I was so desperate to see Rosie again that I didn't know how I would bear to be apart from her another second.

Just then, Cailean came over. "You're in luck," he said. "Fog's lifted."

I looked up and saw that he was right. It seemed to have melted away as quickly as it had appeared.

I scrambled to my feet, eager to get back to the lighthouse and see if Rosie had turned up.

When I thanked Cailean for the tea, he said, "Just don't pull something that daft again."

"Can I walk you back?" Will asked.

I was grateful for the offer. The last thing I wanted just then was to be wandering the island alone at night. Besides, it would give me the chance to tell him about the other odd things I'd experienced at the lighthouse. So I gratefully accepted, and we began the trek back along the cliff path together.

Will listened quietly as I poured out what had happened, and once I'd finished he said, "The Strangers' Room is a focal point somehow. I'm not sure why. Perhaps something happened there once, long ago. Something so awful that it echoes down the years to us."

Before long, the lighthouse came into view, and when we were a short distance away I said, "Thanks. I can take it from here."

Will nodded. "Call for that boat in the morning," he said. "As soon as you can."

It felt like everything had changed between us over the last hour. All my anger towards Will was gone, and I felt only gratitude. We had a shared understanding now and a shared fear of the lighthouse that was reaching up into the dark sky before us. We knew things about it that no one else on the island did, except Rosie, and that made me feel suddenly concerned for his safety too.

"What about you?" I asked.

He paused. "What about me?"

"Why don't you call for a boat too?"

"Guga hunters have been coming to this island for years. Everything's fine as long as no one goes into the lighthouse."

"But *you're* going into the lighthouse," I pointed out.

"Right, but I'm not living there. And I'm not saying the words, so I'm not stirring anything up."

I frowned. "What words?"

Will waved a hand. "Forget it. There are certain words you should never say inside the lighthouse, that's all."

"I still think you should just leave it alone," I said. I didn't like the thought of him staying here and poking about in the lighthouse's dark corners. "You were right – it's dangerous. You still might stir something up so why risk it? It won't change what happened to your sister."

"No, it won't. But I don't want it to happen to anyone else either," Will replied simply. "And if I can put a stop to whatever's going on here then it feels like making amends somehow, to Kenzie. It's my fault that she died here."

"But—"

"Don't worry about me," Will said abruptly. "I'll be fine. Just get your family off this island. And try to forget Bird Rock, if you can." He gave me a small smile. "It was good meeting you, but I hope we never see each other again."

Before I could argue any further, he turned and walked away, back down the cliff path. I let him go. I had to focus on Rosie right now. Even if Dad and Kate had found her – and I prayed that she was safely inside – they must all be panicking that I hadn't come back. When I checked my phone, I saw that almost two hours had passed since I'd left the lighthouse to look for her.

As I carried on down the path, I expected to hear my family moving about outside, calling my name, but the night was completely silent. Perhaps they were off on the other side of the island, looking for me? Maybe they'd left a note. But as I walked past the kitchen window, I glimpsed something that gave me a jolt of pure shock.

Dad and Kate were right back where they'd been before I'd interrupted them – sitting at the kitchen table, playing a card game with Charlie. Everyone looked completely relaxed and I even saw Dad laugh at something Charlie had said. For a moment I just stared, hardly able to believe that they'd let me wander off into the fog and hadn't been worried at all. But it must mean that Rosie had come back at least. I went to the kitchen door and opened it.

They all looked round, big smiles on their faces.

"Oh, hi, Jess," Dad said. "Were you stargazing? Surprised you can see anything on a night like this."

I glared at him. "No, I wasn't stargazing," I snapped. "I was looking for Rosie, remember? What happened? I thought you were going to help me. Has she come back?"

I looked past them to the doorway, hoping to see Rosie there, but it was empty. When I glanced back at the others, they were all staring at me with confused expressions on their faces.

"Why are you looking at me like that?" I asked, feeling more and more annoyed. "Is Rosie home or not?"

Dad frowned and set down his cards. "Who's Rosie?" he asked.

Chapter Fifteen

At first, I thought they were playing a weird joke on me, but then Dad started to get impatient and said, "Jess, honestly, I have no idea what you're talking about. I've never heard of anyone called Rosie."

My head was buzzing so much I thought it might split open. I pushed past Dad and went up to our bedroom, intending to grab Rosie's phone, or her camera, or her crystal collection, but her things were gone – every single one of them. There was no trace of her left. Even the card Charlie had drawn was now addressed only to me, and the little stick figure of Rosie had vanished from the front so that it was now just the four of us. I thrust my hand into my pocket but the crystals I'd taken from the Strangers' Room earlier were gone as well.

Dad and Kate had followed me and were asking questions, but I ignored them and switched on my phone. I had masses of photos of Rosie on there – selfies of us both, of Rosie pulling a face for the camera or grinning beside a pool on holiday, a dollop of ice cream on her nose. But the photos had vanished too. I scrolled desperately but there wasn't a single trace of Rosie on my phone at all. Nothing. It was like I'd never had a sister.

"But this … this is ridiculous!" I said, whirling round to face Dad and Kate. "You can't have just *forgotten* her. That's absurd!"

Dad sighed. "Is this a cry for attention? Have you been feeling jealous of Charlie, or—"

"DAD!" I was shouting now. "I don't want attention – I want my sister! You *can't* have forgotten her, you just can't! Why do you think you went to the guga hunters' camp earlier today? You were cross because Will showed her a video on his phone."

"No, I was cross because he showed a video to *you*."

I shook my head, despairing. "I never saw any video. Rosie was ill a few years ago, remember?

I know you don't see much of us, but you came to visit her in hospital—"

"Jess, that's enough," Dad said, looking as if he was torn between concern and irritation. "*You* were the one who was ill. It's you I came to see in hospital. But all that's behind us now."

I'm not sure how long we argued about it. I know I tore through the house like I was possessed, desperately seeking evidence of Rosie that simply wasn't there. Of course it inevitably came out that the trapdoor was unchained, and Dad and Kate were gobsmacked by the discovery, following behind me as I rushed through the rooms up in the tower.

At one point, I lost it and grabbed Charlie by the shoulders, shaking him, trying to get him to admit that he remembered Rosie. Dad started to get properly angry with me then, but I didn't care. My life was unravelling, so what did it matter if he was angry? I was angry too. And absolutely terrified.

I stormed back outside. Rosie had to be on this island somewhere, and I was going to find her. It was still dark but at least the fog had cleared. Dad and Kate both followed me for a while, talking and pleading, before eventually Kate went back to be with Charlie, and Dad ordered me to return to the lighthouse too. I refused, and when he tried to grab my arm I ducked away and set off at a run down the path, ignoring his calls.

I wandered around Bird Rock for hours. In fact, there was a faint touch of pink starting to stain the sky by the time I finally found myself back at the lighthouse. Its light flashed out to sea, warning people to stay away from the island. God, I wished we'd listened. I was exhausted in every limb, and there was no point searching any more. I'd come close to the guga hunters' camp a couple of times – and Dad had been stumbling around the island calling for me half the night too – but other than that I'd seen no trace of any person at all, including my sister. She'd simply vanished, along with those other people I'd glimpsed in the fog. It was unthinkable and impossible – but somehow it had happened.

As I stared at the lighthouse, I wanted to cry at how right Will had been. There was something very wrong with it. I thought back to the camera going off in our bedroom that night, and the hands I'd seen pressing against the glass downstairs, and the room full of photos, the writing on the walls.

DON'T FORGET!

It couldn't be a coincidence – those words printed over and over again – and now it seemed my whole family had completely forgotten that Rosie ever existed. Not only that, but she had also disappeared – vanished into thin air, just like the missing keepers all those years ago. I was certain that the lighthouse was responsible for what had happened to my sister. My entire body seemed to scream at me to run away from the building and to keep on running, but of course I couldn't. I had to do the opposite and walk straight back inside.

When I finally trudged into the kitchen, I found Dad at the table with an untouched mug of tea in front of him and his head in his hands. He looked up as I opened the door, and I saw that he clearly hadn't been to bed.

"I've radioed the mainland," he said. "Kate will stay here with Charlie, but you and I are leaving this afternoon."

"No."

Dad sighed. "Jess, if you truly believe what you've been saying about a sister, then you're obviously having some kind of breakdown, and I'm just not equipped to handle—"

"I don't," I said, my mind working quickly.

I knew that these next few moments would be vital. I was the only person who could prevent Dad from leaving Rosie behind. If I failed … well, I couldn't even bear to think about it.

Dad paused. "Don't what?"

"I don't believe what I said. About having a sister." It was so difficult to force out the words, like spitting stones through my teeth, but somehow I managed it. "I … I said it to get attention, like you thought."

"Christ, Jess." Dad looked furious. "Is this some kind of game to you? You really frightened Kate and me. Look, I know it's hard being together like this, in each other's pockets, but if you're finding it that difficult then we should still leave."

I took a deep breath. "You're right. I'm sorry. But I really would like to try again. Please."

I waited, holding my breath. Eventually he sighed and said, "I'm going to try to get a few hours' sleep.

I suggest you do the same. We'll talk about this later."

I nodded, doing my best to look contrite. Dad took himself off to his bedroom, and I made my way upstairs. It was barely six in the morning so I expected Charlie to be asleep too, but then I heard a tearing sound, and when I passed his open bedroom door I felt a gust of cool sea air blow through. I glanced inside and saw him standing at the open window. I was just about to tell him to close it before more flies came swarming in, but then I realized he wasn't just standing there – he was throwing something out of the window.

"What are you doing?" I asked.

He jumped and spun round with a guilty expression. He looked like he hadn't slept much either. His eyes were bloodshot and his face was pale. He held half a piece of paper in his hand. I saw it was one of his crayon drawings, like the card he'd given us when we arrived and the ones I'd found outside our room later. I just had time to make out the jagged white wing of a gannet before Charlie screwed the whole thing up in a ball and tossed it out of the window.

"Dad will be angry if he sees you throwing your

drawings outside," I warned.

Charlie glared at me with an oddly mutinous expression on his face. "That wasn't *my* drawing!" he said.

"It doesn't matter whose it is," I said. "Just put it in the bin."

I was about to go to my bedroom, but then I paused and said, "Charlie? I just want to ask one more time, and then I promise I won't again. *Do* you remember Rosie?" I had some faint hope that he might answer differently if it was just the two of us. "It's OK to say if you do," I went on. "You won't be in trouble, I promise."

But Charlie shook his head once again. "I have one sister," he said. "Just one." He gave me a worried look. "Perhaps the lighthouse is sending you mad?"

I sighed. I didn't think I'd ever been so exhausted in my life. "Maybe."

"Jess?"

"Yes?"

"What does it feel like to be mad?"

"I don't know, Charlie. Not very nice, I suppose."

"Would you *know* if you were mad?"

"I don't know that either. But probably not."

I left him to it and returned to my own bedroom. It felt so wrong crawling into my sleeping bag and lying down alone, without Rosie snoring softly beside me, but I eventually fell into a restless sleep with tears on my cheeks.

Chapter Sixteen

Day Six

When I woke up a few hours later, I saw the spot where my sister ought to have been, and the agony of the night before came flooding back. It was even harder to believe everything that had happened when I opened the shutters and filled the room with sunlight. Surely I hadn't really seen ghostly people in the fog? And surely I'd find Rosie taking photos outside? Yet the bedroom was still empty of her things, and when I grabbed my phone there wasn't a single photograph of her on there. It was like she'd just been wiped from existence.

I quickly dressed and went downstairs. Dad and Kate were sitting at the kitchen table and fell silent the moment I walked in. There was an awkward moment before Dad pointed at a chair and said,

"Take a seat, Jess. We need to talk about what happened last night."

Reluctantly I sat down and listened as Dad delivered a lecture about personal responsibility, and acting my age, blah-blah-blah. I gathered that he'd cancelled the boat, but he wanted my assurance that I wouldn't have any more meltdowns. Of course, I had no choice but to promise. Whatever it took to remain on the island and find Rosie.

"Let's all just try to start over," Kate said, leaning across the table towards me. "Jess, tell us how we can help make this easier for you."

"I'd like more time to myself," I said at once. "I feel crowded when we're together too much."

I steeled myself against the look of hurt that flashed across Dad's face.

"But isn't that why you're here?" he asked. "So we can spend time together?"

I shrugged. "I want some time to myself too," I said.

"Of course you do," Kate said calmly. "I'm sure we can find a balance. Right, Nathan?"

Dad's shoulders seemed to slump. "Sure," he said. "If that's what you want."

"I'd like the tower to stay unlocked as well," I went on quickly. "It's nice up there. I find it … peaceful."

I had to force the lie out through gritted teeth, but Dad said, "Well, there's not much I can do about that anyway, as there don't seem to be any spare chains or padlocks around here. Just be careful on the staircase. Kate and I have some work we should do today actually. If we take Charlie with us, then you'll have the place to yourself for the afternoon. How would that be?"

"Sounds good."

I felt bad pushing Dad away but I wouldn't be able to find out what had happened to Rosie if we were together all the time. As it was, I felt a chill touch my blood at the impossibility of the task ahead of me.

Later, we had a subdued lunch. No one was much in a talking mood, even if any of us had known what to say. It didn't help that Charlie kept complaining about there being someone under the table again. He sounded so convinced that I even glanced down myself at one point, but of course there was no one. It was a relief when Dad and Kate finally packed up their equipment, left me with one of the walkie-talkies and instructions to contact them if I needed anything, then bundled Charlie into his windbreaker and went out, leaving me free to return to the spiral staircase and the trapdoor leading to the tower.

I was so much more frightened to go up there this time, but I pushed all that to the back of my mind, heaved the door aside and climbed into the darkness, making my way to the Strangers' Room first. Or at least I tried to – but when I pushed against the door I met resistance. I felt a sudden flare of hope inside my chest. Perhaps Rosie was on the other side? Maybe she'd fallen asleep leaning against it or something. This was the last place I'd seen her so perhaps she was simply back? It wouldn't make sense, but I wouldn't care – I'd just be so happy and relieved to see her again.

I pushed harder at the door, throwing all my weight against it, and this time it opened. Only it wasn't Rosie in the Strangers' Room. There were birds. Dozens and dozens of them forming a white carpet across the floor. The window was open, and I guessed they'd got into the room by mistake, but rather than flapping about in a panic, squawking and shrieking, they were standing completely silent and motionless, all looking up into the curved mirror. I could see their beady little eyes watching me from the warped old glass.

My mind flew back to the last letter I'd found on the back of Charlie's drawing.

It's not an illness like we first thought
— it's the lighthouse...
The birds that get inside the building go mad...
It was like they'd been staring into the mirror for so
long that they'd forgotten they were birds at all...

How was the window even open? I was sure I'd closed it when I'd been up here earlier. There must have been fifty birds in the room. After the disturbing things I'd read about them in those old letters, I felt nervous about getting too close, but they couldn't stay in the lighthouse. So I came into the room, shut the door behind me so they couldn't get to the stairwell, and then began shouting and waving my arms at them.

This seemed to shock them back to themselves, and suddenly they were behaving like ordinary birds again, flapping about, screeching, looking for the exit. It was a large window, and to my relief it wasn't too difficult to usher them back outside. Soon the room was empty again, the only sign of the birds the occasional stray feather, some smears of guano on the floor, and of course their dreadful stink.

I closed the window firmly and then went back down to the room with the photos. They were all still scattered about on the floor where I'd left them, and the writing on the walls seemed to scream out a warning at me – a warning that I had heeded too late.

DON'T FORGET! DON'T FORGET!

Could this have happened before? To one of the lighthouse keepers? Perhaps that was why some of them had been thought mad. Perhaps they alone had remembered a person that everyone else had forgotten. Later that afternoon, I was going to track down Will and make him tell me everything he knew about the lighthouse and what exactly had happened to his sister, but for now I had the logbooks to read.

Surely something in there might help me work out how to get Rosie back.

I quickly realized, though, that it was a daunting task. There had been dozens of lighthouse keepers at Bird Rock over the years – even more than you might expect because so many had requested transfers and ended their terms early.

I found journal after journal filled with dense pages of cramped handwriting. I flipped through them at random to begin with. Many of the entries were pretty innocuous – just recordings of weather reports and fuel levels and sea conditions. But there were strange entries that came up several times. More than one keeper had seen white hands pressed up against windows or mirrors. Many reported weird goings-on inside the Strangers' Room and an unease about the mirror hanging there. And several keepers documented the birds acting oddly, or even violently. Even more alarmingly there were reports of the keepers acting violently towards each other too, in sudden and out-of-character ways.

Eventually I found the log of a man called Gerald Hartley. He'd been one of the last two keepers on Bird Rock in the 1970s, and his partner was John Porter – Cailean's grandfather, whose log I'd already read bits of. When I discovered Gerald Hartley's logbook, I saw that he often doodled little drawings in the margins.

They were pictures of gannets mostly, and sometimes seals or the monks' stone bothies on the other side of the island. But there were also, oddly, drawings of an old woman that started to appear in the pages too. She was a fearsome-looking being dressed in rags, with straggly grey hair that trailed down her back, and crooked black teeth gaping from her mouth. In fact, she was hardly a person at all – her eyes were just dark pits in her face. For some reason, she was always shown kneeling by the edge of a stream, washing clothes. I flicked back to the first drawing of her and read Hartley's accompanying entry.

Dreams at the lighthouse seem to get stranger and stranger. I've never suffered their like before. I'm used to the isolation all right, so I can't think what's causing them. Maybe it's all those shrieking birds? Or the strange thumping I hear most nights from the Strangers' Room?

I frowned down at the page, remembering my own nightmares and unsettled by the reference to the Strangers' Room. The entry continued:

I dreamed of the bean nighe again last night. It looked to me as if she was washing Porter's clothes, but when I attempted to get close enough to check, I couldn't reach her, no matter how hard I tried. The fog kept closing around her, hiding her from my view. But I knew she was there because I could hear her humming — that utterly sorrowful tune...

With a jolt, I recalled the soft melody I thought I'd heard in the fog, just for a moment, last night. I peered closer at the keeper's drawing — a stark charcoal sketch. The woman looked almost inhuman with that snarling mouth and a face that was more like a skull.

It doesn't help matters that Porter has been acting strangely ever since that night of the storm when he claimed to see a pair of *hands at the window. Last night I found him smashing one of the mirrors to bits, and when I asked what the hell he was doing he could offer no explanation for his bizarre behaviour...*

Suddenly I heard a thump down below and froze. Dad had said they were going to be out all afternoon. Had they come back early? The next moment, the door swung open to reveal Will on the threshold.

I breathed a sigh of relief. "Oh, it's you. I thought my family had come back."

"I saw them on the clifftop." Will stepped into the room. "What are you still doing here? I hoped you'd all be gone by now. Didn't you find your sister?"

My heart suddenly lifted. If Will remembered that I'd been looking for Rosie, then might he actually remember her too?

"Do you remember her?" I asked eagerly. "Rosie, I mean."

He frowned. "Well, how can I? I've never met her."

"But you *have*," I said, feeling a fresh wave of despair. "You've spoken to her a couple of times on Bird Rock and caused a big upset yesterday by showing her the video on your phone, remember?"

"But that was *you*," Will replied. "I showed you the video."

I shook my head. Will and I had spoken about the video last night but now that I thought about it I wasn't sure if he'd ever specifically mentioned Rosie or had just apologized for playing it.

"When I got back last night, I found that my whole family has forgotten her too," I said. "But Rosie *does* exist. I travelled to this rock with her all the way from London. She ate at the table downstairs with us and took photos of the lighthouse outside. She was here. She was real. But somehow everyone's forgotten her. I know this must sound completely impossible, but it's the truth."

There was quiet for a moment, then Will said, "It sounds wild but … well, with this place, I think anything is possible. It's hard to accept that my memories aren't accurate, though. If that's the case, then how can we trust anything we think we know?"

I was silent for a moment. "I guess we can't," I finally said.

Will gestured at the words written on the walls. "Perhaps this has happened before. If people were vanishing and being forgotten, then how would we know that they'd vanished? Unless there was someone left like you who *did* still remember. Maybe that's why so many keepers here were considered insane and ended up in asylums."

"Yeah. I had the same thought."

"If this is true, then it makes it even harder to know for sure what's happening on the island," Will went on, looking worried. "Maybe there was originally someone else in the lighthouse with you, or another hunter back at the camp with me, and they've gone, and we've forgotten them already. We can't possibly know what we no longer remember."

I groaned and put my head in my hands. I didn't feel like myself at all. What if that meant it was happening to me too? Maybe it would be my turn to melt away into the fog next.

"What the hell is happening here?" I asked.

"It all stems from this place," Will said. "It's been unlucky since the day it was built."

"When was that exactly?" I asked.

"No one knows. The records were lost, remember? Or never existed to begin with."

"I've just been looking at one of the old keeper's

logbooks," I said. "He keeps drawing this old woman. He calls her a … a bean nighe?"

I held up the book so Will could see. His eyes narrowed slightly at the sight of the old woman on the page.

"It's pronounced *ben neer*," he corrected. "The Washerwoman at the Ford."

"You've heard of her?"

"She's a Scottish myth. A type of banshee. They say she appears beside streams or rocks, washing the clothes of a person who's about to die."

So that was why Hartley had been trying to get close enough to confirm whose clothes she had in his dream.

"Other keepers mention her in their logbooks as well," Will went on. "But that one you have there is the most disturbing because … well, the day after Hartley had that dream, he found Porter dead at the foot of the lighthouse."

"Do you think she's *real* then?" I asked incredulously.

Will met my gaze. "I don't know any more," he said. "Do you?"

I thought of the humming I thought I'd heard out in the fog – so haunting and horrible.

"No," I replied with a shiver. "I'm not sure about anything. But I'm going to find out."

Will's face fell. "But you said you'd call for a boat this morning to get your family off Bird Rock."

"Not without Rosie," I replied. "Look, why don't we work together? We both want to get to the bottom of whatever's going on here. You're the only person on this island who even believes me, the only person I can trust."

"But you can't."

I frowned, confused. "Can't what?"

"You can't trust me. You can't trust anyone on Bird Rock, not even yourself." He paused. "Especially yourself. Not when the lighthouse is awake. I know this is difficult, impossible, but if you really do finally believe that there's something wrong with the lighthouse then won't you even consider leaving with your family? Your sister might still be gone, but at least you'll have saved the rest of them—"

"Not a chance," I said, shaking my head. "I'm not leaving this island without Rosie. I mean it. If I have to chain myself to the lighthouse door, then that's what I'll do. I wasn't asking your permission – and I'm doing this with or without your help."

I took a step back towards the logbooks, but my heel brushed the edge of a lighthouse photo, and suddenly every light in the picture of the tower blazed brightly from the windows.

"What the—?"

I stared down at the photo. The lights in the one next to it all came on then, and all the others around it too, until we were surrounded by dozens of illuminated lighthouses.

Chapter Seventeen

"What the hell is going on with these photos?" I snatched one up from the floor.

"I told you they were cursed," Will replied.

I stared down at the picture in my hand. There was no longer anyone standing in the window. When I looked at the ones on the floor, they were the same.

"There was a person here before," I said. "Standing at one of the windows. I think it must have been the Strangers' Room."

"A person?" Will asked sharply. "Are you sure?"

"Yes. I couldn't see their face because they were backlit, but there was a clear silhouette."

"It must have been them," Will muttered.

"Who are you talking about?"

He only shook his head slightly, so I held the

photo up, peering at the window, half hoping and half dreading the appearance of that dark figure.

"There!" Will said, pointing at one of the photos on the floor.

I looked down and saw that a blurry face had appeared at a window in the tower, just for a moment. Then it vanished, only to turn up in the photo next to it. The same thing kept happening, as if the person was moving through the photographs somehow. And then, all at once, there was a figure at the window in every photo again, including the one in my hand.

"Don't look too closely," Will said quickly. "They don't want to be seen."

I knew there was no point asking him who he was talking about a second time.

"If they don't want to be seen, then why are they looking out of the window?" I asked impatiently. I looked back down at the photo in my hands. "Who are you?" I said. "Why don't you show yourself properly? I know you're there."

My last words had the most extraordinary effect on Will. I heard him suck in a harsh gasp of a breath, and when I glanced at him he looked utterly horror-stricken, as if he'd just seen a ghost. The colour had drained from his face so completely that I wondered if he might actually keel over. Then we both heard the tread of a footstep on the spiral staircase, and Will flinched.

"My family must have come back early—" I began.

"No!" Will's voice was barely more than a whisper. In a few steps, he'd crossed over to me and clapped his hand over my mouth. "No, no, no!" he muttered as he tugged me into the corner of the room.

I shoved his hand away and whirled round to face him. "What the hell are you—?"

"Please!" Will hissed. "Please listen. You've got to be silent."

He turned me round, and I found myself standing so close to the wall that my nose almost touched the peeling plaster, as Will tucked himself in behind me.

"What are you—?"

"Trust me!" Will's voice was soft in my ear. "Close your eyes, and no matter what you hear, don't open them or turn round. For God's sake, do as I say!"

My throat burned with the hundreds of questions

I longed to ask, but the urgency in his voice was unmistakable and I could feel how tense and rigid he was in every limb. So I did as he said and closed my eyes.

Suddenly the door behind us flew open so hard that it banged against the wall and caused a shower of plaster to rain down from the ceiling. Every instinct in my body was screaming at me to turn and see who had just entered the room, but Will curled himself closer around me.

It clearly wasn't a member of my family. This person was silent. All I could hear was the rasping sound of their breath. The floorboards creaked as they came closer and closer, until it sounded as if they must be just centimetres away. The breathing was horribly loud in the room, echoing round it like a wave inside a shell.

I could smell something rank and unwashed and even thought I felt a faint puff of warm breath against my elbow – as if the person behind us was on their knees. Will must have felt it too because he tensed even more. It took every ounce of willpower I had not to whirl round to face the thing behind us. It was only Will's rigid body that kept me from doing so. I could feel how desperately he was urging me not to turn round, so I stayed where I was, but my eyelids trembled with the effort of keeping them closed, and I kept expecting to feel icy fingers dragging me backwards at any second.

Finally, after what seemed like an eternity, the person began to move away. We heard their slow steps retreat across the room and then the bang of the door as they went out. I opened my eyes and would have spun round, but Will whispered, "Give it a moment."

We stayed like that for another five minutes before Will finally glanced over his shoulder and said, "All right. It's safe."

My knees buckled and I sagged against the wall, relief and terror roiling around inside me. "What the hell is going on?" I said, turning to look at Will. "Who was that?"

He was still pale and I could see that the last few minutes had shaken him up too. "You really don't remember watching that video on my phone, do you?" he asked.

"No," I replied. "Because it wasn't me you showed it to."

"All right, well, I think it's about time you saw it. Perhaps then you'll change your mind about wanting to work together. Let's get out of here."

"Can't you just show it to me now?"

"I can't play the video in the lighthouse. Or anywhere near it. The building will know, and it … it won't like it."

I thought of arguing, but after what had just happened, it did sound good to get out of the lighthouse for a while. I nodded and followed him towards the door. He checked to make sure the staircase was clear, and then we both hurried down it, and I left a note for Dad saying I'd gone for a walk.

Despite the birds and the flies and the awful stench of guano, it was a relief to be out in the cool sea air, away from the oppressive atmosphere of the lighthouse. I followed Will as he picked his way over the scrubby grass, taking care to avoid the rocks. Every now and then, I glanced back at the lighthouse, my gaze drawn to it irresistibly, but nothing weird happened. No lights came on, and no faces appeared at the windows.

As we continued along the cliff, we passed close

to the hunters' camp and I saw some of the men in their blue overalls using a system of pulleys to pass large nets of birds from the high plateau, where they'd been plucking them, down to another part of the island, where they had built a series of peat fires on stone hearths.

One of the hunters was taking the headless birds from the sack and cracking their wings – a horrible sound that echoed through the air – before passing the carcasses to another hunter who held each one in the flames for a few minutes. Even from this distance, I could smell the fat that was pouring off the bodies and could see how the fire leaped and sizzled as the droplets dripped into it. The air smelled of singed skin and grease, and the whole thing made me shudder. There were piles and piles of the dead birds below, and the living ones seemed to fill the sky with their shrieks above us, as if they knew what was happening to their companions and were furious.

Will circled the camp and took us to where the island stretched out in a little outcrop. We were at the furthest point from the lighthouse here, while also being able to see it on the opposite piece of land directly ahead of us. A single stone bothy huddled close to the ground. Will said that it had originally been a place for the monks to come to meditate.

He stood back to let me go inside first. The circular entrance was so low that I had to crawl in on my hands and knees. Once inside, I couldn't have stood up without knocking my head on the ceiling, but it was fine for sitting in. Faint beams of light shone through the cracks in the stones, and it took my eyes a moment or two to adjust to the dimness.

My dad had been right – the bothy made the lighthouse seem luxurious in comparison. I couldn't imagine actually living in one of these huts for two whole weeks, with just the rough, uneven ground to sleep on. No bathroom, no lights, no nothing.

I turned to Will. "Tell me what you know about the lighthouse. What happened back there? Who was that in the room with us?"

"I don't know. Not exactly."

"So what *do* you know? Why don't you start with the video you showed Rosie?"

Will took a deep breath. "Are you sure you haven't already seen it? My memory of yesterday is that you came and found me on the clifftop and wanted me to look at some photos you'd taken of the Strangers'

Room. When I realized you were actually *recording* in there, that's when I knew I'd have to show you the video, no matter how shocking and awful it might be."

"It wasn't me," I said in a quiet, firm voice. "It was my sister."

Will sighed and began to scroll through his phone. "All right. Let's say you're right. Last summer I was here with my sister and her friend. We were bored and playing a game of Truth or Dare. And that's how I learned that there's a phrase you must never say inside the lighthouse."

I frowned. "Well, what is it?"

"*I know you're there.*" Will looked sick as he spoke the words. "There's an urban legend – I'm not sure how it started exactly – but it says that if you go into the lighthouse and say *I know you're there* three times then whatever haunts the lighthouse will appear to you."

He ran his hand through his hair, and I saw that his fingers were shaking slightly.

"I've only ever heard of someone managing to say the words twice. God knows what would happen if you actually did it three times. I said the words twice last summer," he said, "and my sister died. It was ... well. Why don't you see for yourself?"

He passed his phone over, and I saw that it was open on a video file.

"I dared my sister to go into the lighthouse," he went on. "She was only supposed to step inside and then come straight back out again, but Kenzie was... She always had to prove that she was the bravest, the most fearless. So she climbed the staircase to the Strangers' Room. Emily and I saw her turn the light on from where we were standing outside. Eventually, we went in after her and ... the video shows what happened next."

I looked down at the screen and hesitated only for a moment before I reached out and pressed play. Whatever horrible thing I was about to see, I knew I had to do it for Rosie. A small, shaky video filled the screen, and I recognized the lighthouse's spiral staircase and Will's voice saying in a dramatic voice, "And now we're almost at the top. Best keep your eyes peeled for ghosts, and spooks and missing keepers."

Out of the frame someone – a girl I guessed must be Emily – groaned. "Will, do you have to?"

"What?" he replied. "We could make a lot of

money if we film a ghost, and the video goes viral."

A moment later, they reached the Strangers' Room, and Will whistled as he stepped over the threshold. "What is this place?"

"And where's Kenzie?"

In the video, I could see both Will and Emily in the large, curved mirror. A second later, I also saw his sister in the reflection when she leaped out from behind the door with a loud shriek. Emily screamed as Kenzie landed on Will's back, causing him to stagger and drop his phone. It clattered over the tiles, landing face up so that it was only recording the ceiling. I could still hear them talking, though.

"Gotcha!" Kenzie yelled triumphantly.

"What the hell, Kenzie?" Will's annoyed voice came through. "You'd better not have broken my phone!"

"That's not funny," Emily said.

"Oh my God, Em, I never thought you'd actually come *in*!" Kenzie replied. "I couldn't resist the chance to get Will back for calling me chicken earlier. He jumped," she went on, with barely concealed glee. "I felt it. You're scared of this place – admit it!"

"Yeah, right," Will replied. "*You'd* jump too if a

lunatic landed on your back!"

He must have reached down for his phone because the picture suddenly righted itself, showing the Strangers' Room and the three teenagers in the mirror.

"You're lucky you didn't crack my screen," Will said.

"Can we just get out of here, *please*?" Emily begged.

"Not until we get something spooky on camera," Will insisted. "We've come all this way. Aren't we at least going to say the words?"

Emily looked aghast, and Kenzie was shaking her head. "Come on, Will—"

He grinned. "Now who's chicken?" He took a deep breath, and before the others could stop him he spoke quietly but firmly. *"I know you're there."*

The moment he spoke, a floorboard creaked loudly somewhere close by. The sound was horribly like the tread of a footstep.

"Oh my God," Emily breathed, staring into a corner of the room. "Don't say the words again, Will. Really, don't mess about with stuff like that."

"Oh, come on!" Will laughed. "You don't actually think a ghost will appear, do you?"

"Of course not," Kenzie said, but Emily was silent.

"Then what does it matter if I say the words? *I know you're there*," Will said again, still grinning like it was all a joke. It was weird to see him smiling. I didn't think I'd seen him do so once since I'd met him.

The moment he'd finished speaking, the light in the Strangers' Room flickered out. One of the girls – I guessed it was Emily – shrieked as utter darkness swept over them, as inky and fathomless as the bottom of a well.

"The window!" Emily cried, her voice hysterical. "There's someone over by the window. I saw them! I SAW THEM!"

Will flicked his phone torch on and pointed it at the window. He was too far away to illuminate it properly, and the shadows seemed to slither around it like snakes. I clearly saw the word **JUMP!** painted on the wall.

"Jesus, Em!" he said. "There's no one there! You probably just saw your own reflection in the glass. Get a grip!"

But Kenzie was staring at the window too, and she was much closer to it than the others. Suddenly something changed, and a look of absolute horror contorted her face. It made her appear almost not human. Her entire body shrank into a cringe as she started to turn towards the others. Her voice was so quiet that I saw, rather than heard, her say, "Oh *God*—!"

And then the torch on Will's phone must have malfunctioned because they were plunged into darkness once more, thick and suffocating. The screen of the phone was completely black, and I could only tell it was still recording because of the sound. It was hard to tell exactly what happened after that. Something – I guessed it was the door – slammed closed with such a loud *BANG* that I could hear plaster raining down from the ceiling in chunks.

Will was calling Kenzie's name, and somebody was crying. There was the sound of scuffling and panting in the dark, and then Kenzie – it *must* have been Kenzie – saying, "Get out! Get *out!*" But her voice sounded strange and different from how it had before. In fact, it was hard to tell who was talking during the next few moments.

"Where's the *door?*"

"There's someone in here with us!"

"Get out!"

"Will, let go! You're hurting me!"

"I'm not touching you!"

Will's phone was jerking around wildly, and every now and then I could catch a flash of light that I guessed was a reflection from the mirror, or moonlight bouncing off the window. The camera was moving so fast that it was hard to tell what I was looking at, but at one point I thought I saw someone standing facing the window. Will must have thought the same because I heard him say, "Kenzie, get away from the window!"

Then there was the sound of breaking glass, so shrill and sudden that I actually jumped. And then … then there was silence. At last, the electric light overhead flickered back on, but now there was only Will and Emily in the room. As the phone jumped round, I could see Emily sprawled on the floor by the marble fireplace, tears running down her face, and Will's reflection showed up near the window that was, quite clearly, broken – shards of glass gleaming in the moonlight. And was that … *blood* glistening on the jagged edges?

"Where's Kenzie?" Will gasped.

He ran to the window. I guessed he'd probably

forgotten that he was still recording by now, and the phone slammed against the windowsill as he peered over the edge. Then there was an awful groan that I guessed must have come from Will, and the screen filled with the image of a body lying crumpled at the foot of the lighthouse. Even from this distance, it was possible to make out her fair hair and a dark pool of blood spreading around her on the flagstones.

Chapter Eighteen

I was speechless for long moments after the video finally came to an end.

"I don't know what to say," I finally said, looking at Will. "I'm so very sorry that happened to you. To all of you."

"Me too. I showed the video to the police," Will said. "I guess I thought it was proof of a haunting. I thought they'd do something about the lighthouse, have it knocked down or at least locked up. But instead it just made them suspicious of me."

"Of you?" I frowned. "But why?"

"You heard Kenzie in the video asking me to let go and that I was hurting her." He looked sick. "I never touched her but *someone* had hold of her in there, and I think they dragged her over to that window and pushed her through it. The police thought it might have been me for a while. I spent hours being questioned by them. They never took it any further in the end, but I think it made my parents wonder how responsible I might be for Kenzie's death. I think it made the whole town wonder…"

I remembered Cailean's warning that I should stay away from Will, and the way that Will's dad had spoken to him back at the camp. It was bad enough losing Rosie, but at least my own family didn't think I was responsible.

"This is awful," I said. "Awful that it happened at all, let alone that people think you're to blame."

"But I am to blame," Will said softly. "It was my fault we were in the lighthouse in the first place, and I'm the one who disturbed whatever's inside. I am responsible. I used to be really close to my dad but now … it's like he can barely stand to look at me, and I don't blame him. I don't blame him at all."

I reached out for Will's hand. "I believe every word you've ever said about the lighthouse. I believe there was some dark presence in the Strangers' Room with you that night, and I'm grateful to you for trying to help us. I'm only sorry I was too stupid to listen."

Will gave my hand a squeeze. "If you were stupid, then I was too," he replied with a small smile. "Emily tried to warn me, but I didn't listen either. I was too sure of myself and what I thought I knew was real or possible. And look, I was wrong earlier when I said you should go home without your sister. Of course you can't do that. Of course you have to stay and try to get her back. And I swear I'll do everything I can to help you. This island has already taken everything from me – if I could swap places with your sister, I would in a heartbeat."

Suddenly I was very aware of the warmth of his hand against mine, as well as our physical closeness as we huddled together in the bothy. I could feel an unwelcome heat prickling over my face. Will must have noticed because suddenly our hands weren't touching any more, and he cleared his throat.

"All that matters now is finding out what's going on with that place so we can break the loop," he said. "I think there's someone or something inside the lighthouse that doesn't want anyone else in there with it. You and I both know there was a person in the room with us earlier. Kenzie was the only one out of our group to see them properly last year, and she was the only one who died. I think that whoever's there doesn't want to be seen, and if you *do* see them then it's too late."

"That's why you told me to close my eyes," I said.

"Yes, although it wasn't just a hunch. Something similar happened to one of the other keepers. I read about it in his logbook. He described hearing footsteps while sleeping in the Strangers' Room one night, and for some reason that he couldn't explain even to himself he knew he shouldn't look. So he pretended to be asleep. He described how the figure came right up close to him, and that there was a smell, a bad one, but when he kept his eyes closed the person eventually went away. The keeper requested a transfer the next day, but he was convinced that not opening his eyes had saved his life. Every logbook I've read suggests that all the keepers knew there was something wrong with the lighthouse and the Strangers' Room especially."

"And that's it?" I asked, feeling a dark sense of hopelessness wash over me. "That's all you know?"

"For now," Will replied. "It's hard to find out much on the mainland. The Northern Lighthouse Board don't really like to talk about Bird Rock. It's a stain on their record, I suppose. Whatever information remains is here on the island – in the logbooks themselves and any other documents that are still being stored here."

"And the writing on the walls," I added.

I glanced at my watch. "My family will probably be back soon. Perhaps you could come tonight, after they're all in bed? Then we can carry on going through the logbooks. I'll make sure the kitchen door is left open."

Before Will could reply, we heard a yell from outside – a piercing scream of fear that sliced through the air around us. In a flash, Will and I were both scrambling out of the stone bothy. The shout came a second time, and then a third, cutting through the ever-present shrieking of the gannets. We only had to run a short way along the cliff path to see what all the commotion was.

Will's dad stood in the middle of a storm of birds. They all seemed possessed, diving at him with the same terrifying speed I'd witnessed out on the water. I never would have believed that birds could move so fast. They were swarming in such a thick cloud that it was impossible to keep my eyes on Will's dad for more than a moment or two, but I heard him cry out again, and then an arc of blood curled through the air, spattering over white feathers.

Will and I both ran towards them, shouting. We were quickly surrounded by birds as we reached Will's dad. To my dismay, I saw that he was bleeding from gashes on his arms and face. The next moment, a gannet torpedoed towards us and ripped a chunk of hair from his head.

There were so many of them and they were so big that they could do real, serious damage. I trembled as I thought of those letters on the back of Charlie's drawings, and the bird attacks they'd described. The next second, I cried out as one of the gannets flew at me in a frenzy of talons and feathers. I raised my arm to protect my eyes and felt a white-hot slash of pain slice across my skin and warm blood running down my arm. I reached down to grab some rocks from the ground, and Will's dad did the same. The birds started to thin out a little to avoid the stones we hurled at them, but it wasn't enough, and I got the sense that they were regrouping and would be back with greater force at any moment.

I looked around for Will, but just then there was a

loud, echoing bang, like a gunshot cracking the air in two. An explosion of red sparks appeared above us, and the birds quickly scattered. Within seconds, they'd retreated to the cliffs, and it was like the whole thing had never happened. I saw Will standing beside his father's bag, holding a flare gun. He quickly dropped it and came hurrying over. We all had cuts – they were deep and mine throbbed – but I didn't think they'd need stitches. It could have been a whole lot worse.

"What happened?" Will asked. "Dad, are you OK?"

His father was panting slightly, but he nodded. "Thanks to you two."

"Why did the birds behave that way?" Will asked.

"Christ knows. Never heard of such a thing in all my years of coming to Bird Rock."

I thought again of the weird letters I'd found. The claim that the birds, like the humans, had been affected after they'd been inside the lighthouse. And hadn't I found the Strangers' Room packed full of gannets just this morning?

"There's first-aid supplies back at the camp," Will said. "Come on."

The other hunters met us halfway there, drawn by the flare signal. We were soon back at the camp, and I felt out of place in all the noise and confusion that followed. The adult hunters found it hard to believe what had happened, yet they could see the evidence of the bird strike with their own eyes.

"But the gannets have never attacked us before," Cailean kept saying. "It's not their natural behaviour at all. Something must be wrong."

While several of the hunters discussed various bird diseases and their symptoms, the others were fetching bandages and seeing to injuries. Another hunter came up to me with a first-aid bag and introduced himself as Lenny. He had a kind face and set about washing and bandaging my cut arm.

"Sounds really scary," he said, once he'd finished. "I'm sorry you had to experience that, lassie."

I had a horrible feeling that my dreams were going to be full of birds for the foreseeable future – if I was ever able to manage to sleep again, after all that I'd learned today.

It was getting late, so I made my excuses to Will and slipped away, back to the lighthouse. As I approached the tall white tower, I knew at once that my family were already back. Not only was there a light glowing in the kitchen window of the keeper's cottage, but Charlie was hanging from his bedroom window again, throwing out more paper.

He saw me as I got closer and immediately disappeared but there was paper flying about everywhere, all with bright smudges of crayon on them. He was ripping up his own drawings again. The gannets were swooping through the debris eagerly. Perhaps they thought the paper was food – many of them were gobbling down the little shreds, while others were flying off with bits of paper lodged in their beaks.

After what I'd seen on the clifftop, I didn't want to be around those birds for long, so I hurried inside. Dad and Kate must have only just got back because they were organizing their equipment in the entrance hall. I said hello and then headed straight upstairs to Charlie's room.

His door was closed, and there was no reply when I knocked, so I opened it, only to be met with an alarming scene. Every single inch of the walls was covered in crayon drawings. Not only that but they were stuck all over the floor and the ceiling as well.

There must have been hundreds of them. When had Charlie had time to do these? And how had he got them on to the ceiling? My brother was tearing round the room like a little tornado, snatching up the drawings and scrunching them in his fists. There was a sort of wild panic in his eyes, and he looked a bit sick.

"Charlie, what is this?" I asked, walking in and closing the door behind me. "Why are you ripping up your pictures?"

I looked at the nearest wall properly then and realized that the childish drawings were all like the one I'd found outside my bedroom the other day. They were filled with gannets but the birds weren't just flying around – they were attacking people. You could tell by the screaming mouths of the little stick people, who were also waving their arms over their heads, and the stark red blood splatters that filled the air. A couple of the gannets were flying off with an ear or a finger.

I thought of the bird attack from that afternoon, and the gash on my arm throbbed.

"Why have you drawn the birds like this?" I asked.

"They're not *my* drawings!" Charlie exclaimed,

231

echoing what he'd said that morning.

"Well, whose are they then?"

He didn't reply but continued racing round the room, ripping up the paper, so I went over and grabbed hold of both his arms.

"Charlie," I said. "Stop for a minute. Look at me. If you didn't draw these, then who did?"

He stared down at the floor, his lower lip trembling slightly. Finally he looked up and said in a whisper, "Did you ever have a secret friend? One you weren't allowed to tell anyone about?"

I frowned. "Well … I had an imaginary friend once. He was a giant rabbit called Podge. Is that the kind of thing you mean?"

But Charlie was already shaking his head. "No," he said. "It's not like that. It's not like that at all."

"Why don't you tell me what it *is* like then?" I asked. "Look, you can trust me. I promise I'll believe you, no matter how strange it sounds."

Charlie paused and for a moment I thought he was going to confide in me. But then he shook his head and said, "Just kidding. I drew them really. It's dangerous to go outside. The birds have gone mad. We've got to stay in the lighthouse. If we go out, the birds will tear us to bits and gobble up our insides."

He held up a drawing for me to see, and I shuddered at the sight of birds eating someone's guts. I assumed it was meant to be one of the guga hunters because they were wearing blue overalls. They were lying on the floor with their pink intestines trailing out on to the ground like eels, while the birds gathered round, crowded together as if they were at a buffet.

"Did you see the birds acting strangely when you were out with Dad and your mum today?" I asked.

But Charlie seemed to have finished talking. He wriggled free of my grip and went back to scooping up the drawings. As he did so, I saw there was faded writing on the back of them and realized that these were more letters.

"Charlie, where did you *get* these?" I asked, snatching a handful from the wall. When I flipped them over, they were all covered in the same neat handwriting I'd seen before.

"Don't take those!" Charlie said. "They don't belong to you!"

"Where did this paper come from?" I asked again.

Charlie paused, then spoke in almost a whisper.

"My friend gave them to me. But I'm not supposed to talk about it."

I tried to prise further details from him, but it was no use – he clammed up completely. Finally I left him to it and went upstairs to check the Strangers' Room. After what had just happened, I wanted to be sure there were no more birds in there but, to my relief, the window was shut and the room was empty.

For some reason that I couldn't explain to myself, I took a few steps closer to the mirror. It seemed like a magnet, drawing me in, and I suddenly felt the strongest temptation to stare into the glass as Rosie had done and see if I experienced that same feeling of losing myself… I tore my gaze away with an effort. I wanted to rescue Rosie, not end up trapped and forgotten alongside her. So I went downstairs to where Dad and Kate were having a cup of tea in the kitchen. Or at least Kate was. Dad was emptying one of the cupboards for some reason, pulling all the tins out on to the kitchen worktop.

"Hi, Jess," Kate said brightly. "Did you have a nice time this afternoon?"

"Sure," I replied. "Until a whole load of gannets

attacked one of the guga hunters on the clifftop."

"Don't be silly! Gannets don't attack people," Dad said, still rapidly emptying the cupboard of tins.

"These ones did," I said, annoyed that he was immediately dismissing what I'd said. "Didn't you see anything like that today? Charlie said something about the birds going mad so I thought maybe you'd come across some odd behaviour too?"

Kate shook her head. "Not that I noticed. I mean, a gannet might squawk at you a bit if you got too close to its nest. Sometimes they'll regurgitate their food too, as a defence mechanism to see off potential threats. Is that the kind of thing you mean?"

"No! This was a proper bird attack. They were swooping out of the air and tearing bits of hair off the hunter. They turned on me when I tried to help too – look."

I unwound my bandages to show them the cuts on my arm. That got their attention at last – Dad finally stopped rummaging in the cupboard, and they were both horrified.

"Thank goodness you weren't more badly hurt," Dad said, his face ashen. "I've never known gannets to act like that."

Kate put her arm round me. "I'm so glad you're OK."

She helped me reapply the bandages, then said, "We'll have to make sure Charlie doesn't go outside by himself from now on. In fact, perhaps both of you should stay in the lighthouse?"

I shook my head. That was definitely *not* what I wanted. "I can't stand being cooped up in here," I said. "I'm sure it'll be OK. I can always take an umbrella or something to keep the birds away."

"Nathan, what do you think?"

Dad didn't reply. He'd gone back to the cupboard and was rooting around in it again.

"Nathan?" Kate said a bit louder. "Are you even listening? What are you looking for in there?"

"What?" Dad sounded distracted.

"What are you looking for in that cupboard? You've practically emptied it."

"Oh. I've lost something important. I'm just checking to see if it's in here."

I stared at the tins piled up on the worktop and the almost frantic way in which Dad was pulling out more. Suddenly the logbook came back to me – the one that mentioned a keeper who was always looking for something, but didn't seem to know what he'd lost. Could this be happening with Dad now? Might he be searching for Rosie without realizing that's what he was doing?

"What have you lost, Dad?" I asked.

He froze suddenly, a tin clasped in his hand. Then he turned round, and there was an odd look of confusion on his face. "I haven't lost anything, Jess." He frowned. "I thought I had but … I must have made a mistake."

Perhaps his subconscious did remember Rosie on some level after all. But that still wasn't much help to me.

"What do you think about the children leaving the lighthouse?" Kate pressed. "Given what Jess has just told us?"

"I'm sure it'll be fine," Dad said, staring vaguely into the cupboard.

Kate looked a bit annoyed by Dad's feeble response, and I didn't blame her. "I think we should talk about this more later," she said firmly. "But for now I'm going to tell Charlie to stay inside. And could you put all those tins back where you found them, please? I had them organized in a system."

She went off, leaving me in the kitchen with Dad. He was still just standing there, staring into the empty cupboard.

"Dad?" I finally said. "Are you OK?"

He hardly seemed to hear me, and when I repeated the question he just waved his hand in a distracted way and said, "Not now, Jess."

There didn't seem much point trying to interact with him. As usual, he was no use to me at all, so I took myself off to the bathroom. After being in the middle of the gannets like that, I felt as if I could smell them on my clothes and skin, and I desperately needed to wash it off.

To my irritation, the shower wasn't working properly – barely a dribble of water came out – so I ran the bath instead. It looked like no one else had used it since we'd been here because I had to clear out the dead bugs first, and the taps squeaked when I turned them on. A whole load of rust-coloured water came out before it finally ran clear.

I groaned and suddenly felt a ferocious pang of longing to be back home, soaking in my own bath, listening to my favourite playlist on my phone, with Rosie hammering on the door, demanding to know how much longer I was going to be. The thought of Rosie and normality was too painful, and I quickly pushed it away. I couldn't think about my sister and our home right now. If I did, then I'd break down completely. So I just poured a generous glug of the bubble bath I'd brought into the tub and went back to my bedroom while it filled up.

When I came back a few minutes later, the bath was almost full, with a great frothy pile of bubbles floating on top and the familiar scent of orange blossom filling the air. I quickly stripped off my clothes and sank into the tub. There were so many bubbles that I couldn't even see the water, but it felt amazing to soak in the clean, scented warmth.

I scooted further down so that the water lapped against my shoulders, then leaned my head back and closed my eyes. My head was a whirl of gannets and ghosts, and I longed to rest my buzzing brain for a moment and think of nothing at all.

I'd only been in the bath for moments when something cold, smooth and leathery brushed against my leg.

Chapter Nineteen

I jerked upright, my hands sloshing water over the side as I gripped the edge of the bath. In the first confused moments, I thought a flannel or piece of soap must have fallen in, but then I felt the thing brush against my waist, and something thick and heavy glided straight over my stomach. There was something in the water with me. Something alive.

I let out a yell of horror, splashing water everywhere in my desperate attempt to get out, but when I went to stand up my foot slipped on something solid and muscled, causing me to fall backwards, plunging into the water, which closed right over the top of my head. A drowning person getting sucked into a stormy ocean could hardly have felt more panic than I did in that moment, especially as my tumble seemed to send whatever was in the water with me into a frenzy.

There must have been dozens of the things because I could feel their cold, smooth little bodies all over my hands, feet and legs, coiling and curling around me. Then I felt the ripping bite of sharp teeth tearing into the flesh of my thigh, an excruciating pain that made me scream, even though I was still underwater.

I must have swallowed half the tub but eventually I managed to haul myself over the side, landing in a shivering heap on the bath mat. Blood ran down my leg, and I trembled in every limb as I dragged myself to my feet. My eyes went straight to the bath, and so many of the bubbles had splashed on to the floor that I could finally see what had been in the water with me.

There weren't several creatures as I'd first thought – just one massive one. It was an eel, easily a metre and a half long and as thick as a human thigh. It was still thrashing and flailing in the bathtub, exposing the white of its belly. As if sensing me watching, it opened the jaws of its rounded snout, revealing row after row of razor-sharp conical teeth.

It's a nightmare, I told myself, trembling. *It has to*

be, it has to be, it has to be. I would wake up at any moment…

Only I didn't. The bathroom floor was icy cold beneath my feet, the blood was warm on my leg, and I knew that I was awake, that this was really happening. I snatched up the towel and backed away until I hit the sink. The next second, cold fingers brushed my bare shoulder, and I spun round.

A pair of white hands stretched right out of the old mirror – actually stretched right *out* of it this time, not merely pressing up against the glass like before. The fingers clutched at the air as if they were trying to grab me, more and more hands suddenly filling the warped glass behind them.

I tried to scream but my chest ached with the effort of attempting to force out air, and only the faintest breathless wheeze escaped my lips as I turned and fled the room, almost colliding with Kate out on the landing.

"Jess!" she exclaimed. "What in the world? Are you all right?"

I was still shaking from head to toe – even my lips were trembling, so it was hard to get the words out at all.

"Th-there are hands in the m-mirror and an eel in the … the bath."

Kate gave me a look of total bafflement. "A what?"

I didn't repeat myself, just grabbed her hand and dragged her into the bathroom.

The mirror looked perfectly ordinary once again, not a single hand in sight. There was water all over the floor, and as we approached the tub I was suddenly very afraid that the eel might have vanished too. Dad and Kate would say that I'd cut my leg shaving or something. They'd think I was losing my grip on reality and I'd start to think so too. Perhaps I might even begin to wonder whether they were right and that I'd never had a sister at all, that Rosie was just a figment of my imagination, that I was the one who'd been ill, that there was nothing wrong with the lighthouse, only something wrong with *me*… But when I pointed at the water, the great dark shape was still there, so big and thick and muscled that it filled up half the tub.

Kate let out a sound that was half gasp and half moan. "Oh my God!" She gripped my arm. "How did it get in there?"

When she fetched Dad, he said that it must have

got in through the pipes and slithered out of the tap.

"But it's as big as my thigh!" I protested. "How could it possibly have squeezed out of the tap?"

Dad pinched the bridge of his nose, looking suddenly tired. "I don't know, Jess. Perhaps eels can make themselves really small in order to fit through gaps like that? It could be a sort of survival mechanism. A mouse can fit through a space the size of a pencil head, you know, and—"

"That isn't a mouse – it's a whacking great sea monster!" I shouted, suddenly losing my temper. I was just so sick of being doubted all the time, of no one ever believing me or helping me.

"Well, for God's sake, what do you want me to *do*?" Dad snarled.

I didn't think I'd ever seen him snarl before, and I didn't get the chance to reply before he lunged towards me. For a shocked moment, I thought he was going to hit me – something else that had never happened – but instead he snatched the bin up from the floor and hurled it at the mirror so hard that it shattered into sharp little fragments that flew out all over the tiles in glittering pieces.

After what had happened with the hands earlier,

I half expected to see people standing where the mirror had been, but of course there was only the curved brick of the lighthouse wall. For the next few moments, there was a strange, strained silence, although I kept hearing the mirror smashing on a loop inside my head. Dad looked more shocked than any of us and gaped at the mirror as if he couldn't believe what had just happened.

Before I could say a word, Kate exploded at him in anger. She was absolutely furious and lectured him for ages about how someone could have been hurt, and she wouldn't put up with any violent outbursts. Dad looked terrified beneath the force of her wrath, immediately returning to his usual mild-mannered self as he apologized to us both with a pained look of shame. But all I could think was that it hadn't been him – not really. Dad never behaved like that. I'd never seen him lose his temper once in my whole life. It was the lighthouse affecting him somehow. Hadn't other keepers mentioned similar things in their journals?

I felt a cold chill of fear touch my blood. Was history repeating itself? First Dad had been emptying out the cupboards, looking for something he couldn't name, and now this. Would he be jumping from the top of the lighthouse next? Or hurting one of us?

After what seemed like ages, everyone had finally calmed down a bit, but I didn't mention the hands I'd seen in the mirror again. What was the point when I knew full well that no one would believe me? It was agreed that we would all wash using the basin or shower from now on, and of course all our drinking water came from bottles anyway.

I thought I would never have a bath again for as long as I lived, and certainly not one with bubbles in it. Even once I was out, it felt as if the eel was still there, sliding and slithering over my skin, and I kept thinking I could feel its long body in my sleeves or the legs of my jeans. Luckily, the bite to my thigh wasn't as bad as it had looked to begin with, but it still stung like anything and I was in a miserably bad mood by the time the four of us sat down to dinner.

I felt Rosie's absence like a physical wound and kept glancing at the chair where she ought to have been. It was even worse because no one else knew she was even missing. The only person who looked as wretched as I felt was Charlie, who once again refused to touch his food. Perhaps feeling the tension of the evening herself, Kate finally lost her patience with him and ordered him to eat the microwaved pie on his plate.

"I can't eat in here, Mummy," Charlie replied in barely more than a whisper. "There's something bad coming up through the floor. It makes me feel weird."

"Charlie, we can't go on like this. You haven't had a proper meal since we arrived at Bird Rock. You must be starving. You're not leaving this table until you've had your dinner – I mean it."

It was painful watching Charlie try to eat that pie. Anyone would think he was consuming something putrid and rotten, the way his eyes watered and his face grew steadily pale.

"I don't like it!" he said. "It tastes like eel!"

"Charlie, you wouldn't even know what eel tastes like!'" Kate replied. "Please just finish your dinner. You're not getting down from this table until you do."

So Charlie carried on taking tiny baby bites of the pie. He was still only halfway through by the time we'd long finished. Finally he laid down his fork and said, "Please, Mummy, can I go to my room?"

"Not until you've—" Kate began, but that was

as far as she got before Charlie leaned forward and vomited all over the table.

Kate and I immediately leaped to our feet. I expected Dad to do the same, especially as he was the one sitting closest to Charlie, but weirdly he remained where he was, gazing out of the window, as if he wasn't aware of what had happened. In all the commotion, Charlie shot off to his bedroom, and between us Kate and I soon had the mess cleaned up.

"I just don't know what to do about this, Nathan," Kate said, as she took her seat. "I thought it would settle down after a while, but it's getting worse. Look, perhaps Charlie and I should go home early? He can't just not eat dinner for two weeks. Nathan? Are you even listening?"

Kate sounded frustrated, and I didn't blame her. Dad wasn't paying any attention at all. He was still looking out of the window, frowning.

"Are we ... are we expecting a visitor?" he asked.

"What?" Kate stared at him. "No, of course not!"

Dad turned to her, his face troubled. "Oh. We're not? But ... I thought I saw somebody out there. And someone else is supposed to be here, aren't they? What's happened? Where have they gone?"

My breath caught in my throat. Surely he was talking about Rosie without realizing it?

"It's just us, Nathan," Kate snapped. Then she seemed to remember me and gathered herself. "Sorry, Jess," she said. "But I think I need to speak to your dad by myself."

"I was about to turn in anyway," I said. "Goodnight."

"Goodnight," Kate replied.

Dad said nothing. He was staring out of the window again.

I made my way upstairs, intending to check on Charlie. As I got closer to his room, I could hear a weird crunching noise coming from inside. The door was closed but I pushed it open without knocking and then froze in shock in the doorway.

"Charlie!" I gasped. "What are you *doing*?"

Really, I ought to have asked *why* rather than what. I could see plainly enough what he was doing. He was eating his pet snails. The crunching sound I'd heard was their shells breaking between his teeth. Charlie jerked round at my voice. Tears were streaming down his cheeks, and there was a terrible look of shame on his face as snail

249

juice dribbled down his chin.

"I don't want to!" he wailed, bits of shell falling from his lips. "I don't want to eat them! But I'm so hungry!"

Suddenly I remembered how he had tucked into the food during our picnic and that time he had asked me to bring him a ham sandwich in the middle of the night, and I realized that the food itself wasn't the problem – it was being in the kitchen. My eyes went to the tank, but I saw that it was empty. He'd already eaten all the other snails.

"Look, I've got some crisps and chocolate bars in my room," I began. "Would you like—?"

That was as far as I got before he leaped to his feet and rushed past me, straight into my room. As I followed him in, he was already grabbing the snacks from my bag and tearing into them.

I let him eat in silence for a few minutes. Then I said, "Once Dad and your mum are out of the kitchen, do you want me to go and make you a sandwich and sneak it up here? Perhaps a couple of biscuits too?"

His face brightened and he nodded eagerly. There was some colour returning to his cheeks already.

"All right," I said. "I can talk to your mum tomorrow too and persuade her that you should have your food somewhere else. You won't have to eat in the kitchen again. But Charlie, I'm only going to do that on one condition. You have to tell me why you don't want to be in there."

His face fell, and he immediately started shuffling his feet and avoiding my eye.

"It's your choice," I said. "But if you don't talk to me then I'm not fetching you that sandwich."

"It's not the kitchen," Charlie said miserably. "It's the room underneath."

"You mean the basement?"

Charlie nodded. "Something happened in there," he whispered. "Something bad."

"Is this to do with the secret friend you told me about?"

Charlie glanced at the doorway, as if afraid there might be someone there, watching us. Then he looked back at me and said in an even softer whisper, "There's a boy. In the lighthouse. With us."

Rosie's voice echoed back to me.

I think I just saw Charlie in one of the tower windows...

"No one's supposed to know about him," Charlie

251

went on. "Except I'm allowed cos we're friends. He hides in the basement during the day. Then at night he goes up into the lighthouse. I think he's looking for his daddy, only he's afraid of the birds."

"Birds?" I thought of the letters. "Charlie, is this the same friend who gave you those old letters?"

Charlie nodded slowly, his eyes huge.

"He says he found where his daddy had been keeping them inside the secret hole in the wall upstairs. It's where he found the tin soldier too. He brought the letters back and draws pictures for me on them. But I don't like the pictures. They're scary."

"All right, but Charlie, who is this boy? What do you know about him?"

"Nothing," Charlie replied. "Just that his name is Conall. And sometimes he wants me to go into the basement with him, but I won't."

"What does he look like?"

"I don't know."

"But if you're friends with him then surely—?"

"He won't let me see his face!" Charlie cried. "He never lets me see it. And I don't know if we *are* friends. I thought we were at first, but now

252

… sometimes he scares me. He wants me to do something bad."

Before I could ask what, Kate came upstairs to check on Charlie and tuck him in. As soon as she and Dad went to bed, I sneaked some more food in to my brother, like I'd promised. He refused to talk any more about his secret friend, so once I was sure everyone was asleep, I tiptoed back downstairs to unlock the kitchen door. The fog had swept in again. It wasn't as bad as before and I hoped Will would still come. I hated the thought of going into the basement alone. To my relief, he arrived soon afterwards. I ushered him into the kitchen and closed the door.

"Is everything OK?" I asked. "Have there been any more bird attacks?"

Will shook his head. "No. Nothing out of the ordinary. How about here?"

I closed my eyes for a minute. Where did I even start?

"There … there were hands reaching through the bathroom mirror for me," I said, shivering as I recalled the sight of them. "And an eel in my bath."

He stared at me. "*What?*"

I told him what had happened.

"Dad thinks it must have got into the pipes and squeezed out through a tap. I didn't see it until I got in because of all the bubble bath."

Will looked appalled. "But ... you don't mean that you were *in* the bath with it?"

I nodded. "It bit my leg before I scrambled out."

"Jesus, Jess! That's ... how are you even still in the building after that?"

I swallowed. "I can't leave. Not without Ro— Without Ros—"

I faltered as a sick feeling of horror swept over me. What was her name? Suddenly I couldn't remember it. Was it Rosalyn? Rosemary?

"Rosie?" Will said, watching me closely. "You told me her name."

"Yes!" I gasped. "That's it! Rosie!"

"You forgot for a moment, didn't you?"

I felt a hot wave of shame prickle over my skin. "Oh God," I said miserably. "Eventually I'll forget her too."

I quickly told him about Dad's weird behaviour, how he had smashed up the mirror.

"I don't like it," Will said, narrowing his eyes. "There's too much talk in the logbooks of other keepers acting in similar ways, usually before something horrible happens. We're running out of time. Let's head up to the tower."

"Actually, wait," I said. "Do you know if any of the lighthouse keepers ever brought their families with them? Has there been any mention of children in the logbooks you've read? A boy called Conall?"

Will slowly shook his head. "Not that I've seen. Keepers did take their families sometimes, but I guess Bird Rock isn't the most suitable place. I haven't been through every single logbook, though, so there could be a child I'm unaware of."

I told him what had happened with Charlie and the letters I'd read.

"Rosie thought she saw a boy in the lighthouse too," I said. "And you know when we were in the photo room earlier and … and there was something in there with us? I thought they were shuffling on their knees because I could feel their breath on my elbow, but what if they weren't on their knees, just shorter instead? What if the presence in the lighthouse is a child?"

"Could be," Will agreed. "Either way, it's pretty interesting what the letters said about the lighthouse affecting the birds. That would explain why we don't normally notice any strange behaviour from the gannets when we come for the hunt. If the lighthouse is shut up, then they wouldn't get inside it. And we should definitely take a look at the basement."

I led him back out to the entrance hall. The basement door loomed out of the darkness at us, and I hesitated. Every cell in my body screamed at me not to go down there after what Charlie had said. Or at least to wait until morning. But the fact that I'd just forgotten Rosie's name for a moment proved there was no time to waste.

"Come on then," I said.

I reached out for the door before I could change my mind. It swung slowly open to reveal a stone staircase disappearing down into murky darkness.

Chapter Twenty

My fumbling hand found a light switch on the wall just inside. I flicked it, and to my relief a yellow electric light came on. It was weak, and flashed on and off a bit, but it was better than trying to use our phone torches on the stairs. As someone who'd always lived in a London flat, the idea of having a basement at all was already pretty weird to me. There was a damp smell that seemed to have soaked into the stones themselves as we descended.

I found another light switch at the bottom of the staircase and flicked it on, my whole body braced for ... I don't even know what. But when the light filled the room we saw that it was empty except for an old backup generator. The fact that there were no windows made it seem cramped and claustrophobic, but that was all there was to it. It was just a room.

"Perhaps Charlie was making it up," I said. "It's not even underneath the kitchen, is it? The stairs led straight down, so this room must sit beneath the entrance hall."

We poked into the dusty corners a little more, but it really didn't seem as if there was anything here to find. No writing on the walls, nothing. I couldn't work out whether I was disappointed or relieved as we made our way back upstairs. I checked to make sure Dad and Kate weren't around, then Will and I quickly returned to the tower.

"Look, these are the letters I told you about." I pulled out the ones I'd taken from Charlie's walls earlier, and Will and I read them together. They were similar to the one I'd read before – nightmare accounts of birds that had become dangerous. The boy was clearly terrified of them.

"Let's take another look at the Strangers' Room," I said.

One way or another, it was the focal point to all this. Kenzie had spent her final moments there, and it was the last place I knew Rosie had gone too. My eyes went to the window as soon as we walked in, and I saw that there was an object on the window ledge. It was the little tin soldier Charlie had been playing with before, staring straight out through the glass, as if contemplating the grisly instruction painted on the wall. Had Charlie been up here again? I slipped the toy into my pocket before turning my attention to the rest of the room.

When I took a closer look at the horrible graffiti encouraging people to jump, I noticed for the first time that someone had dug gouges into the panels too, in the form of words:

GOD FORGIVE ME.

Now that we looked more closely, several of the panels had been carved with this message. They were faint, and clearly old, and you had to look hard to spot them, but they were there.

Will frowned. "I wonder what this person had done?"

"Charlie mentioned something about a secret hole in the wall where Conall found the letters," I said. "He said it was in the tower somewhere. Perhaps in this room?"

I ran my hands over the panels, searching for any loose edges, and Will did the same. One of the panels hung slightly loose, so didn't take long to find. It shifted beneath my hand and I gripped the edges, working it free to discover a small recess behind it.

"There's something back here." I reached in and my fingers closed around a pile of dry paper, the top one of which was a letter. I held it out so that Will and I could both read it.

Dear Mr Jackson,

We regret to inform you that your son Conall has committed the grievous crime of murdering a workhouse warden, and has therefore been sentenced to death. The execution will take place next Thursday week at noon. No visits to the condemned will be permitted, but you are duly informed as his next of kin.

Regards,

Overseer of the West Dean Workhouse

Will and I both stared at the letter.

"It doesn't make sense," Will said. "I'm familiar with

all the names, and there's no record of any keeper named Jackson ever having been stationed here."

"Perhaps he changed his name?" I suggested. "We know his son wasn't executed because he was here on Bird Rock. Look, what's that writing at the bottom?"

We both squinted at the letter. There was indeed more writing there, but it had been written in pencil rather than ink and was so faint that it was hard to read. We could only just make it out.

The confession of Finn Jackson.

God forgive me for keeping my son locked in the dark. For lying to him about his mother still being alive. And for the great betrayal I must now commit.

As God is my witness, I can think of no other way.

"Finn was the name of one of the first keepers," Will said. "Finn Lewis. So maybe you're right.

Perhaps he changed his surname. He obviously got the boy out of the workhouse before his execution somehow. Perhaps he took the keeper job at Bird Rock to hide from the law?"

"If the boy was here in the lighthouse," I said, "then what happened to him? His father must have kept him hidden from the other keeper somewhere. In his letter, he mentioned being locked in the dark, so perhaps he was kept in the basement?"

"Maybe. But surely the other keeper would have had to go into the basement sometimes to check the generator?"

Neither of us had any answers.

The other papers were more letters from Conall, and we took them with us back to the photograph room. Will dug out Finn Lewis's logbooks while I went through Conall's letters. They made for grim reading. All addressed to his mother, they detailed his time in the workhouse, when his father fell into debt. It sounded like a viciously cruel place. He described being ravenously hungry all the time, as well as the various punishments for even the most trivial offence. I could hardly believe the brutality.

One night, I was really bad and wet the bed. When the master found out, he strung me up from the ceiling in a sack and I had to stay there all night...

They made us kneel on wire netting covering the hot-water pipes...

Beaten with stinging nettles...

Head rubbed into the wet coal on the floor...

When the master grabbed me that morning, I was afraid of what he would do, and lashed out without thinking. I broke his glasses and he fell backwards over the bench and struck his head on the stone flagstones. There was a lot of blood on the floor. It was an accident, Mama, I swear it.

They were going to take me away and kill me, but Papa came to get me.

We came to Bird Rock, and now I have to be very quiet because no one can know I'm here. Daddy says he didn't know there was going to be another keeper, but he arrived a little while after us, and he can't know I'm here because he used to work as a warden in the workhouses, and he wouldn't understand. He wouldn't be on our side.

It's so dark and cold here, Mama, and the storms are scary. I hope I can see you again soon. Your loving son...

I put the letters down. They made my chest ache, and I didn't want to read any more. I quickly filled Will in before asking if he'd learned anything from the logbooks.

"Nothing about the boy, but look at this." He was frowning down at a piece of paper. "I found it in one of the logbooks. It's—"

But that was as far as he got before we heard a loud banging coming from downstairs. We both froze. It was past midnight. What could possibly be making that noise? We scrambled to our feet and Will thrust the piece of paper he'd been looking at into his pocket.

"You'd better stay here," I said. "Dad and Kate will be awake by now too."

But Will was already shaking his head. "There's no way I'm letting you go down there by yourself."

He followed me out of the door and back down the spiral staircase. We'd just reached the landing when I heard Dad's bedroom door open downstairs, and then the light in the hall came on. Finally I realized what the banging was. Someone was knocking at the front door. For a wild moment of hope, I wondered whether it might be Rosie, and I hurried to the top of the stairs eagerly as Dad threw open the door. But it wasn't Rosie. It was Will's father.

"I'm looking for my son," he said. "Is he here?"

"What?" Dad's hair was sticking up everywhere, and he sounded still half asleep. "Of course he isn't."

"Well, he's not at the camp," Will's dad said. "And I can't think where else he'd be."

Dad turned towards the stairs, and with a sinking feeling I knew there was nowhere to hide. His eyes fell on me and Will at once.

"Dad, I can explain…" I began.

But Dad wasn't in the mood for explanations. In fact, he was furious. Predictably Will was thrown out at once, giving me a hopeless look as he left. The door closed on him and his father, and I groaned in frustration. Time was running out and now I'd lost the one person on the island who was trying to help me get Rosie back. I could have strangled my dad, especially when he absolutely refused to listen to a word I said.

"Will's been helping me look into the lighthouse's history," I said for the hundredth time. "That's all."

"I had no idea you were such a history buff, Jess,"

Dad said in a sarcastic tone. I guessed it *did* sound pretty flimsy, especially since I couldn't tell him the real reason I wanted to learn more about the lighthouse in the middle of the night – at least not in a way that he would believe. "No wonder you wanted Kate and me out of the way."

Kate tried to stick up for me, but I could tell that her heart wasn't really in it, and when Dad finally stopped raging at me and I returned to my room, I paused at the top of the stairs and heard Kate say to Dad that perhaps we should all leave Bird Rock.

"It just isn't working here for the children," she said.

Dad sighed. "Maybe you're right. I'll radio for a boat first thing in the morning. We can be back on the mainland by the afternoon."

A sense of sick panic filled me. I couldn't leave Bird Rock. Not without Rosie. I suddenly had an image of my life continuing as normal in London, except for the gigantic hole where Rosie should have been. I'd need to save the money to get back to Bird Rock by myself, somehow organize a boat to get here, and, realistically, it could be years before I returned, and would I even still remember Rosie by then? I was running out of time – I had to do *something*.

I waited until I could hear no more movement from downstairs, then, treading quietly, I went down to the kitchen, unplugged the radio and slipped it into my bag. With the radio gone, Dad wouldn't be able to call for a boat. I turned towards the door, and that's when I saw the hands – pale white hands pressed up against the door's glass panel.

I stood and stared at them, my own hands trembling where they gripped the straps of my bag. When I'd seen them before, I'd assumed there must be a person attached to them, standing out of sight in the darkness or hidden within the warped glass of the mirror, but this close to the window I could see that there was no one beyond. There were only hands pressed so hard against the glass that I could see the veins running through the skin.

My breath seemed too loud and ragged in my ears as I stared at them. I knew that I wasn't the first person at the lighthouse to have seen them, but I still had no idea what they meant. It felt like I was no nearer to discovering the truth about anything than I had been since the day I arrived, and a great rush of despair crashed over me.

But the despair made me angry too, and the anger

made me feel less afraid, so I walked right up to the door and pushed it open. I expected the hands to move back with the door, or else to melt away into the night, but instead they came right through the glass, breaking it with a smash. I stared in horror at two hands poking through the jagged pieces of glass – dark red blood pouring over the white skin. But the worst thing about it – the *worst* thing – was how the hands trembled and reached out towards me, as if silently pleading for help.

I ran. Even if I'd been brave enough to stay, I was afraid the breaking glass might have woken Dad and Kate. So I slipped out of the door and set off along the cliff. I didn't dare turn my torch on in case I was seen, but my eyes quickly adjusted to the moonlight, and I hurried along as fast as I could. I paused to look back at the lighthouse just once. There was a light on, near the top of the tower in what I guessed was surely the Strangers' Room, and I saw a figure standing there, just for a moment. Then it was gone, and the light winked out.

Sea mist settled around my shoulders, along with a sense of hopelessness as I went across the island to the bothy Will had shown me – the one that was a little apart from all the others. As I walked, a couple of stone cairns loomed out of the darkness, looking like people for a split second before my eyes adjusted. I dreaded seeing those motionless figures once again.

Even the hunters' camp was quiet when I skirted around it, and I arrived at the bothy without coming across another living thing. I swung the bag from my back, took out the radio and paused. I could try hiding it – but this wasn't a large island, and I was afraid Dad would find it. His words from the day we'd arrived came back to me:

It's literally our lifeline to the outside world…

If I got rid of it, then we wouldn't be able to call for help in an emergency. But who was I kidding? What help could anyone give us out here on Bird Rock anyway? It would take hours for a boat to get here, and even then no one would believe a word about haunted lighthouses and forgotten sisters. There was no aid I could expect from the outside world, so I drew back my arm and threw the radio as hard as I could over the side of the cliff. It sailed down into the dark sea and was immediately swallowed up by the night and the hungry waves.

For better or worse, it was done. I glanced up into

the night sky and, just for a moment, thought I saw that pale blue man outlined by stars once again, only from this angle it looked as if he had one greedy hand stretched out towards the lighthouse... I blinked hard, and the constellation vanished. I knew the stars and the night sky for this part of the world at this time of year, and there was no such figure. Yet the idea of there being murderous blue men hidden in the ocean below no longer seemed as preposterous to me as it had before. Perhaps Will was right, and they had cursed the lighthouse after all. Perhaps that was why this place was so messed up.

Suddenly I couldn't face the long trek back to the lighthouse, and it had started to rain anyway, so I crawled into the bothy instead. If I was back early, then no one need know I'd been gone. I did my best to make myself comfortable by using my bag as a pillow. The ground was cold and hard, but I was exhausted and fell asleep within seconds.

It was still dark when I jerked upright, trying to work out where I was and what had woken me. Then I heard the humming.

The sound chilled my blood, just as it had the first time out in the fog. So haunting and other-worldly and sad. It sounded as if it was coming from right outside the bothy. I turned towards the entrance, only to freeze. The stone archway was full of gannets. They were packed in shoulder to shoulder, like sardines, all completely silent and motionless, all staring in at me with their shiny, beady eyes. My breath caught in my throat at the sight of so many behaving so unnaturally.

"Shoo!" I cried in a shrill voice, hurling my bag at them. "Get out!"

I had no idea what I'd do if they flapped inside, but to my relief they scattered, squawking indignantly. I could still hear the humming as I grabbed my bag and crawled from the bothy, the little bits of rock and gravel digging painfully into my knees and palms. The rain had stopped, but the wind had picked up, meaning that the mist from before had blown away, and I could clearly see the woman hunched just a short distance from my hut.

She had her back to me but I heard the splashing of water and saw at once that she was washing some clothes in a large puddle that had formed between the rocks – all the time humming that sad, slow song to herself. Every cell in my body screamed at me to run from the woman, but I knew who this was – it was the bean nighe. I was seeing her as previous lighthouse keepers on the island had before me. And I was desperate to know whose clothes she was washing.

So I swallowed down my fear and picked my way over the rocks towards her. The air seemed to get colder and colder as I approached, so cold that it suddenly felt difficult to imagine ever being warm again. Up close, the woman was even thinner and frailer than I'd first thought. The hands grasping the clothes were more like claws, with long, dirty yellowed nails. Her skin was withered and pale, her shoulders sunken. She had the look of a creature that lived below ground and never saw the sunlight. Her wiry grey hair was so patchy in places that I could see the wrinkled white skin of her scalp, especially as the wind practically howled around us now, as if it would tear every hair from her head.

"Go away!" she hissed, although I hadn't spoken a word. "Lot to get through before sunrise."

She gestured at something with her bony elbow,

and I spotted another set of clothes on the ground beside her. My breath caught in my throat as I realized that the puddle had already turned red with blood as she energetically wrung out one of the blue boiler suits the guga hunters wore. Since they all dressed alike, it was impossible to tell who it belonged to.

The outfit beside her, though, was another story. I recognized that dark jacket – the moonlight flashed off the tiny silver football badge pinned to the pocket. Those clothes belonged to Will. Without even thinking about it, I started forward towards them.

"*Don't!*" the old woman hissed, still wringing out the boiler suit.

Her tone made me shudder. I dreaded seeing her face but I couldn't let her have Will's clothes. I lunged forward and my hand closed around his jacket, but the bean nighe was upon me lightning fast.

Her face was barely human. Her skin had shrunk so tightly around her skull that I could see the bones pressing through. Her eyes were black, gaping holes. The rotting teeth in her mouth were needle sharp, her lips were cracked and dry, and so were her hands

– the skin peeling red and raw from all that washing.

"That isn't yours!" she hissed at me.

Her grip on my wrist was surprisingly strong, and I cringed at her touch. Her skin was wet and wrinkled – she felt like a thing that had been in the water too long.

"It's not yours either!" I snapped.

She grabbed the jacket and pulled. I tightened my hold, and the material ripped, one small piece of fabric from the shoulder still clutched in my hand. I lunged for the rest of the jacket, but the bean nighe shoved it beneath her ragged shawl, out of reach. Seeing that I still held a piece of the jacket, the old woman leaped on me with a furious cry. Her body looked small and frail yet was surprisingly heavy as she crouched on my chest, squeezing all the air from my lungs. Her wiry hair fell across my face and I scrabbled backwards over the ground, my spare hand searching for a rock to hit her with. But then the bean nighe gave a sudden hiss of anger and I realized she was looking towards the lightening sky rather than at me.

"Useless girl!" she spat, shoving me away and gathering up the remaining clothes. "That scrap won't change anything. I'll wash somewhere else."

With that, she half crawled, half dragged herself towards the bloody puddle. To my astonishment, she threw herself into this as if it was a lake, and the puddle closed over her head and swallowed her up. When I ran over, I saw that she'd vanished completely, and the water was clear and shallow once again, only a few centimetres deep.

The bean nighe had gone but in my hand I still gripped a scrap of Will's jacket. I stared down at it for a moment before shoving it into my coat pocket and zipping it up. I was about to turn away when her bony, wrinkled hand shot right out of the puddle, grabbed my ankle and, with one sharp yank, dragged me beneath the surface, the bloody water closing over my head.

Chapter Twenty-one

Day Seven

I woke up inside the bothy with a start, gasping for breath. A nightmare. Of course that was all it was. Just a dream. Only it didn't feel like one. There were no fragments of jacket inside my pocket but I couldn't shake the feeling that what I'd just seen – whether inside a dream or not – was somehow real. There were surely a hundred different ways a person could meet their death on this island, especially if they were a guga hunter clambering down cliffs and hanging over ferocious open fires and skinning birds with very sharp knives. For my own peace of mind, I decided to check in on the hunters' camp before heading back to the lighthouse.

The cliff path was thick with gannets, and I had to dodge round them as I went. It was almost 6 a.m. by the time I reached the camp, and I could see that the hunters were already up and about. It looked like they were busy storm-proofing everything, covering the bothies with weighted tarpaulins and moving away some of the equipment. A horde of gannets perched on the nearby rocks, watching the proceedings with interest, but nothing seemed out of the ordinary, and I tried to tell myself that all was well. I was just about to leave when I spotted Will. I waved at him, and he came over at once.

"Jess, I'm so sorry about my dad," he began. "I hope you didn't get into too much trouble with your family? I was going to come over first thing and explain to them that we were only—"

But I cut him off. "It doesn't matter now. Dad's threatening to call a boat to take us back to the mainland so I threw our radio in the sea."

"He wouldn't have got a boat here today anyway," Will said, pointing up at the sky. "Another storm's blowing in."

"Oh. Well, at least he can't call for one tomorrow then. Listen, something happened as I was leaving the lighthouse."

I told him how I'd slipped away in the night and

seen the white hands at the door, trembling as they bled through the glass.

He shook his head. "Jess, you've got to get out of that place. I know you want to find Rosie, and I understand that, but—"

"But nothing!" I snapped. "I'm not leaving Bird Rock without her. And there's something else I need to tell you. I feel a bit stupid mentioning this, but I had a horrible dream about the bean nighe last night. She was washing a guga hunter's boiler suit and she was ... she was washing your jacket as well. I managed to snatch it away from her and tore off a small piece."

"I'm sure it was only a dream," Will replied slowly. "But Jess? If you have any more like that, don't try to approach the bean nighe again, OK? Even in a dream, it's—"

But that was as far as he got before the gannets descended upon us in a furious storm. As one, they spread their two-metre wingspan and dived into our midst at that unbelievable sixty miles an hour speed. It didn't look natural to see birds move that fast, and their beaks gleamed like pale grey blades. Their shrieks were even shriller and louder than usual as they flew at the hunters in a frenzy. It was hard to tell what was happening amid the cloud of white wings, but I saw blood spray out through the air, along with human hair. Everyone was running and yelling, making their way towards the shelter of the stone bothies.

I raised my arms to protect my head from a gannet racing past, felt the brush of feathers against my skin. Will was shouting something about getting to a bothy. But then it happened. One of the hunters was only a few paces away – it was the man who'd introduced himself as Lenny when he'd bandaged my arm the day before. We saw the bird dive directly at him, but there was nothing we could do to help. The bird hit the side of his head, beak first. We heard the crack of bone, and Lenny went down as if he'd been shot. The gannet fell limp and lifeless beside him, and we realized that the impact had killed it.

Will and I raced over, dropping down next to him at the same time as Cailean crouched on his other side. A small piece of Lenny's skull had been punched straight through into his brain. His eyes were open and glassy, and there were just a couple of spots of blood on the collar of his blue boiler suit.

But he was certainly dead.

I looked up, and my eyes locked with Will's. I saw raw fear in them as my own words came back to me:

I had a horrible dream about the bean nighe last night...

She was washing a guga hunter's boiler suit...

As if this was the moment they'd all been waiting for, the birds took off, returning to their clifftop perches with their gory human trophies. I didn't want to look at Lenny's body and turned away, only to see my dad hurrying towards me over the rocks and calling my name. He said he'd come to see if I was at the camp when he realized I wasn't in the lighthouse and had arrived in time to witness the bird attack.

"Are you all right?" he asked, gripping my arms tightly. "I'm sorry I didn't believe you about the birds before."

I nodded but his apology was useless. If he didn't believe me about Rosie, then he couldn't be any help.

At least no one else had suffered serious injuries. Lenny's body was covered with a tarpaulin, but I couldn't get the image of it out of my mind. After seeing the bean nighe, I felt responsible, as if I should have been able to do something to prevent his death. I should have taken the nightmare more seriously. It was hard to believe that it was a mere coincidence. I glanced over at Will, and the thought of the same thing happening to him made me feel sick. I could only hope that the scrap of jacket I'd managed to take would be enough to change his fate.

Any animosity between Dad and the guga hunters had now vanished. No one had ever seen the gannets, or any bird, behave like this before, and so having an ornithologist on the island was suddenly a good thing. Dad used his walkie-talkie to let Kate know what had happened and told her not to go outside or let Charlie near the windows.

Not knowing if the birds would come back, we all retreated to the bothies. We had to split up to fit inside, and Will and I went with my dad and Cailean. The wind was even stronger now, and we could hear it howling around the bothy like a lost creature. I could tell Dad didn't know what to make of the bird attack. His best guess seemed to be that the birds were suffering from some temporary madness as the result of eating something poisonous.

"When it works its way out of their system, then hopefully they'll return to normal," he said. "If it doesn't kill them first."

Will and I exchanged a glance. I wanted to tell Dad that it wasn't something the birds had eaten, it was the lighthouse, but I knew he wouldn't believe me, and neither would Cailean.

"For now, I don't think there's much we can do other than hunker down and barricade ourselves against them," Cailean said.

There was some talk of everyone returning to the lighthouse, but as it was on the other side of the island the adults agreed it was too risky, and that the best thing was to stay put. Cailean radioed the mainland to explain what had happened and ask how soon a boat could be sent. I was gutted that getting rid of Dad's radio hadn't made any difference, but at least the people on the mainland replied that no boat could leave just now. The storm blowing in was due to hit Bird Rock this evening and would hopefully have blown itself out by the morning. As soon as possible after that, rescue boats would be on their way.

"It's not so bad then," Dad said. "The storm will keep the birds away too. We just have to get through the night, that's all."

Will and I exchanged a glance. We'd known it was

coming but now it really seemed as if time had run out. What on earth were we going to do?

"You and your daughter are both welcome to stay, of course," Cailean said. "Much safer than attempting to reach the lighthouse."

"I think we should go back, Dad," I said at once. "It doesn't feel right leaving Kate and Charlie there alone—"

But that was as far as I got before we heard a voice shouting outside. When we removed the bags we'd used to block up the entrance, we saw Kate running into the camp, Charlie clinging to her like a monkey.

"They're inside the lighthouse," she gasped, as we ushered her into the bothy. "The gannets. They broke the windows. I've never seen anything like it, Nathan! Some of them cut themselves to ribbons on the glass, trying to get in."

She and Charlie were able to get out in time, although the other walkie-talkie had been dropped and lost somewhere along the way. Neither of them was hurt but Charlie's eyes were as big as saucers, and he looked truly wretched. He kept staring at me too, for some reason, and although I offered him what I hoped was a reassuring smile he didn't smile back.

"We just ran all the way here," Kate said.

"Well, now that we're together, this is where we stay, I reckon," Cailean said. "The bothies don't have windows to smash, and beaks can't break through stone, no matter how much of a frenzy those birds are in. We just have to make sure the entrances are properly blocked."

Will and I could only watch in dismay as bags and equipment were used to fill the little doorway in our bothy. Charlie sidled over to me while this was happening, and I thought he might want to tell me about the gannets, but instead he began mumbling something that didn't make any sense and that I now find hard to remember. Listening to him made my head ache, and I was pretty distracted anyway.

If tonight was our last night on the island, then I had to get back to the lighthouse, no matter what it took. I wracked my brain all afternoon for excuses, but it seemed impossible. The bird attack had so traumatized everyone that they wouldn't hear of people going outside, and there was even talk of digging a hole in the bothy and everyone using that as a toilet. The bothy was too small for me to talk to Will without being overheard, but I could see

that his mind was going over and over it, the same
as mine.

The gannets were strangely absent as the afternoon
wore on. It was odd not to hear their raucous cries
outside. I'd been longing for quiet since we arrived,
but now the sudden silence seemed unnerving.
Dad suggested they could probably sense the
approaching storm and had gone off to find shelter
in the sea caves. Fortunately this meant that the
adults agreed it would be all right for us to leave the
bothy to use the outhouse, as long as we were quick.

I saw my opportunity but knew I'd still have to
wait until everyone else was asleep. Otherwise they'd
wonder where I was after a few minutes and come
to check. Now that Kate and Charlie were here,
there wasn't quite enough room for everyone to lie
down inside our bothy, so it was agreed that Will and
Cailean would each squeeze into a different house
with the other hunters. I thought about trying to say
something to Will before he left, but there were too
many people around and I couldn't work out what I'd
say to him anyway. Meet me later? Don't meet me?

The thought of returning to the lighthouse all alone in the middle of the night was utterly horrifying, but I didn't really want Will to come with me either. Not after that business with the bean nighe. So I said nothing as he left and forced myself to settle into a very boring and subdued evening with my family.

Everyone was uncomfortable and miserable in the stone hut. We couldn't light a fire or have a hot meal, although Cailean gave us some spare sleeping bags and cold food from their supplies. Time dragged, and I was relieved when Kate finally suggested that we should all lie down and try to get some rest. It sounded very quiet in the rest of the camp, and I guessed the guga hunters had done the same. No talking, no birds, no flies, not even a breath of wind. If it wasn't for the strange crackling feeling in the air, it wouldn't have seemed like the start of a fearsome storm at all.

I longed to sneak out as soon as possible, but knew I'd have to time it carefully. If I tried to leave too early and was caught, it could set me back hours. So I lay there in the dark and waited, and waited, and waited. I felt exhausted but didn't think there was much chance of accidentally falling asleep.

I was way too tense for that: afraid of going back to the lighthouse, yes, but — even more than that — afraid of what would happen if I couldn't find Rosie. This was my last chance.

Finally I heard my family's breathing deepen one by one around me and was pretty sure they were asleep. I gave it another half an hour, just to be sure, before deciding I couldn't wait any longer. With my heart beating wildly, I crept across to the bothy's entrance and began carefully removing the items we'd packed into the doorway. When I first looked outside, I realized that another thick fog had rolled in, which perhaps explained why everything had such a silent, smothered feel. It would almost have been better if the birds had been shrieking. At least then there'd have been some noise. As it was, every scuffle and scrape I made seemed amplified in the dark.

When I had created a hole big enough to crawl out, I began to squeeze my way through. I'd almost made it when a hand clamped down suddenly on my ankle. I bit back a yelp and turned round to see Charlie, his face white as he stared at me, his small hand still clutching my leg.

"Don't go out there, Jess," he said quietly.

I winced and shushed him. "Go back to sleep," I whispered. "I'll be right back – I'm just going to use the outhouse."

"No, you're not. You're going back to the lighthouse."

I sighed and scooted a little closer to him. "I have to go," I said. "I left something important there."

Charlie's face crumpled and tears filled his eyes. "You'll vanish," he said. "You'll vanish too."

He reached for my hand, and his little fingers were clammy in mine as he gripped tightly and began to talk rapidly and earnestly.

It's impossible to recall now exactly what he told me, but I remember saying, "Yes, I promise. Now go back to sleep. And don't tell Dad or your mum where I've gone, OK?"

Charlie nodded, suddenly seeming to accept that I was going. He crawled back to his sleeping bag and I quickly blocked up the entrance again before scrambling to my feet. It was a very thick fog, almost as bad as the one that had swept in the night Rosie went missing. Still, fog seemed pretty tame to me now compared to all the other things I'd witnessed on this island, so I straightened my shoulders and set off. There was no sign of Will, either in the camp or the path leading away from it, and I couldn't work out if I was relieved or disappointed. Probably a bit of both.

I knew Bird Rock pretty well by now and found it easier to pick my way back to the lighthouse, using my phone torch to keep an eye on the path. I kept a nervous eye out for gannets, but didn't see so much as a feather. There were no people in the fog either, but all the while the stillness seemed to press down on me like a physical weight.

When I first spotted the beam of the lighthouse's huge lamp flashing through the fog, I almost had the sense that it wasn't a lantern up there at all, but a giant eye sweeping its gaze across the island, searching for me. As I got closer, I saw with a shudder what Kate had meant about the gannets. Many of the windows were smashed, and I could see bloodied birds hanging from the broken glass with limp, broken wings. Kate hadn't closed the door behind her when she and Charlie had fled, and I could hear it squeaking as it moved back and forth in the breeze.

All of a sudden, I thought I could feel a chilly

malevolence pouring from the tower, as if there was someone looking at me from one of the windows. The last thing I wanted to do was go inside, but I had no choice if I hoped to get my sister back.

I walked forward. The ground around the lighthouse was littered with dead birds. As I approached, I tried very hard not to think about how the dark, open doorway looked like the gaping mouth of some monster that would swallow me whole if it had the chance. I took a deep breath and stepped over the threshold.

Chapter Twenty-two

It was dark but the moon shone in through the broken windows, providing enough light to see by as it glittered over the smashed glass. I turned round to close the door, but then froze. There was one unbroken window in the entrance hall and now my eyes were stuck to it like glue. White hands pressed against the glass – not just one pair, but dozens, as many as would fit. I hurried over towards the door and almost collided with the figure coming through. He cried out and I realized – to my relief – that it was Will.

"Bloody hell, Jess! You scared the crap out of me!"

"The hands are back!" I said. "Did you see anyone out there?"

"No, there's no one."

I pushed past him and ran round to the window, but it was empty. I could make out the imprint of the hands, though, and held my fingers up to the cold glass. A moment later, Will joined me.

"I was hoping you'd stayed at the camp," he said. "But I'm not surprised you didn't."

"Same." I turned to face him. "Look, you really shouldn't be here. Not after that dream I had about the bean nighe."

Will shook his head. "For all we know, it was still only a dream. Besides, there's something I need to tell you—"

But that was as far as he got before the clouds above us finally burst, and rain poured down in sheets. The wind rushed back with a vengeance, slamming the lighthouse door closed and tugging the bloodied feathers from the gannets impaled on the broken windows. The storm had finally arrived.

"Let's get inside," Will said, raising his voice above the noise.

We ran back to the door and tumbled into the hall, where I quickly switched on the light. The less time spent in the dark in this place, the better.

"I have an idea about where we need to go," Will said, pulling a piece of paper from his pocket. "I found this in the tower yesterday, just before my dad arrived and messed everything up."

He held it out to me and I saw that it was an architectural plan. "We know that the lighthouse is actually a tower within a tower, right?"

"Right," I said. "From when they strengthened it in the 1800s."

"Well, these are the plans for how they intended to build the second tower. And look." He pointed to a spot on the page. "It looks to me like part of the old basement is still there – the one from the original lighthouse. And it's directly underneath the kitchen."

"You're right," I said, staring at it. "But how do we get to it?"

And should we?

The words seemed to hang in the air, but neither of us spoke them aloud.

"They've labelled it *cold storage*," Will pointed out. "As if they intended it to be used for food. So perhaps there's access through the kitchen?"

Charlie's words at the dining table suddenly came back to me.

I thought there was someone down there. I heard them scratching...

"I think I know where it might be," I said.

We went into the kitchen and flicked on the light, to immediate shrieks of alarm. A couple of gannets had managed to make it into this room alive, and they hissed at us threateningly. Luckily they didn't seem in a fit state to attack us. They'd both damaged their wings coming through the window, and when Will opened the door they were eager to escape into the night, despite the wind that howled in.

"We should move fast," Will said, glancing at me. "There could be more gannets inside."

Together, we grabbed hold of the big wooden table. The wind roared through the broken windows, plucking feathers from the dead birds and swirling them around us. I winced as one landed on my shoulder, leaving a smear of sticky blood.

I wiped it off, and then Will and I dragged the table across the wooden floorboards with a horrible screeching noise. But there was nothing there.

"Perhaps it's somewhere else in the room?" Will said, looking around.

We started to search. The lights flickered a few

times, the rain blew through the broken windows in icy sprays, and we were both soon damp and shivering. But there was no sign of any trapdoor.

"There's got to be a way down there," Will said. "Maybe the entrance is outside. Or perhaps you access it through the basement we were in before?"

"Maybe," I replied. But my eyes were still fixed on the floor where the table had been.

"I really feel like it's right here, though." I dropped to my knees and ran my hands carefully over the wood.

There was one plank that didn't feel quite as flat as the others, so I dug my nails into the edges and tugged. It came free in a cloud of dust. We were able to remove several more floorboards after that, and there, at last, was the trapdoor. You could tell just by looking at it that it was part of something even older than the rest of the lighthouse. The wood was dull and dark, the silver hoop in the middle rusted with age, and there were two large metal bolts fastened across it.

Something about it made a cold sweat break out on the back of my neck. It felt wrong in the same way the white hands at the window had been wrong. Perhaps Will sensed it too because we both moved back, away from the trapdoor. The wind howled outside, sounding alarmingly like a person, and I could feel the hairs rising on my arms.

"It's locked from the outside," Will said, staring down at it. "As if it was meant to keep something in."

I longed to run from that trapdoor. To get out of the lighthouse and never look back.

As if sensing my thoughts, Will suddenly took my hand. "You don't have to do this," he said softly. "You can go. Back to your family."

For a moment, I thought he was right. I wondered why I was even considering opening that trapdoor. Why on earth would anyone open it? But then it came back to me. Someone was missing. My sister. It took a moment but I finally managed to grab hold of her name. I held on with all my might, determined not to lose it again.

"I'm going down there," I said. "For Rosie."

Will sighed and squeezed my hand. "Me too," he said. "For Kenzie."

I slid the bolts back before wrapping my fingers around the metal ring. It was icy cold to the touch, like taking hold of a dead person's hand.

I glanced at Will. "Ready?"

"Ready."

I heaved, and the trapdoor fell back against the floor with a bang, revealing a dark square just narrow enough to fit down. Will nudged me and pointed at the trapdoor. I glanced at it, and a shudder ran through me. The underside was covered with deep scratches, as if someone had tried to claw their way out.

I heard them scratching…

When I looked closer, I saw that there were dull red stains, faded almost to brown, on the wood too. At that moment, with a final flicker, the lights went out.

"Damn." Will switched on the torch of his phone. "It's the storm."

I nodded, desperately hoping that it *was* the storm and not something else. We stared at the dark space leading underground. I peered into the gloom but could see nothing except for the first few rungs of a ladder attached to the wall. I knew if I looked at it for any period of time I would lose my nerve, so I swung my legs over the side and gripped the ladder. Will immediately protested that he ought to be the one to go first, but I ignored him and started

297

to climb. The air coming up felt so cold that I thought it would be a long way down, but I soon reached a stone floor. I kept thinking I'd feel cold fingers on my neck at any moment so I was eager to press my back against the damp wall rather than have it facing an unknown space.

As Will came down to join me, my phone torch swept the room. It was small, barely bigger than a cupboard, there were no windows or doors, and I felt instantly claustrophobic. A terrible, bleak hopelessness seemed to fill the room. There was a single wooden table in one corner and, beneath it, a pile of mouldy old blankets that were now little more than rags.

As my eyes adjusted to the dark, I realized that there was a single piece of paper and a pen on the table beside a stub of candle. I walked over, Will close behind me. The paper was another letter, in the tidy handwriting I'd come to know well.

Dear Mama,

I hope you get this letter, but I don't think you ever will. Something has happened. I've been alone a long time. I was really hungry for a while, but now my tummy just feels like it's shrunk away to nothing. There was a bad storm — the worst one I ever heard — and my last candle will run out soon too.

Papa said he was leaving, but I didn't believe him. I thought he'd come back once the storm was over. He never did. Everyone else has forgotten me. I'm not getting out of this room.

One of the pipes burst, it flooded down here, and an eel came. I know Papa said they were dangerous, but perhaps I could make friends with it? I know it's what I deserve, but being on my own makes me so sad sometimes. And an eel friend is better than no friend at all. Please don't forget me. Don't forget me, don't forget me.

Love from your son,

C

The letter fell from my hand. Will and I stared at each other, aghast.

"He was down here?" Will whispered. "All alone?"

I was about to reply when a hand shot out from beneath the table and wrapped itself tightly around my ankle. I screamed and stumbled back. "Someone grabbed me!"

I looked under the table, expecting to see a person crouched there, but there was only a blanket.

I leaned down, yanked it away and immediately wished that I hadn't.

Curled up on its side was the small, sad skeleton of a child.

Chapter Twenty-three

The skeleton was so little – the boy couldn't have been much older than Charlie. I felt a painful rush of sympathy. No child should be left alone in a place like this. It was monstrous.

"It must be his ghost haunting the lighthouse," I said.

A noise made us both jump, and Will and I turned in time to see a pair of small feet disappear up the ladder. I had the sudden fear that the trapdoor would slam shut above us, and we'd hear bolts sliding across, sealing us inside and dooming us to share the boy's fate. I raced up the ladder and pressed my hand against the wooden floorboards just as the trapdoor dropped closed on top of them. Pain shot through my fingers, and I yelled, but didn't remove them. Instead, I pushed against the trapdoor as hard as I could, flinging it back.

When I stuck my head up, there was no sign of anyone in the room, although I thought I heard the ring of footsteps on the spiral stairs beyond. I lost no time scrambling out of the hatch, then reached down to help Will do the same.

"I think he's gone up into the tower," I said, nodding towards the doorway. "I heard him on the stairs."

We glanced at each other. Were we going to follow him? Even though he'd just been a little boy who had suffered a short life of numerous cruelties, I shivered with dread at the thought of going after him, yet what choice did we have?

We followed upstairs. I was relieved that the lights flickered back on as we did so, but when we opened the trapdoor it was only to find the tower full of birds. A few of them burst through the opening in a flurry of feathers and claws but, without the ability to dive from a height, they couldn't build up any speed. When we peered up into the tower, we saw hundreds more there, their bright beady eyes staring down at us from the shadows.

It was a long and difficult climb. Fortunately the

gannets seemed to take fright at being in such a small space, and many of them flapped off out of the broken windows to be swallowed up by the storm. Those that remained watched us silently from the bannisters, their eyes shining in the dark.

Sheets of rain lashed in, making the stairs slippery, and my heart sped up in my chest as we neared the top. It wasn't only the ghost I dreaded – my fear of heights was making me feel panicky too. I knew the tower probably wasn't going to come crashing down, but it was hard not to think that it *could*, especially with the wind and rain howling so savagely around it.

We looked into the Strangers' Room, but it was empty, so we returned to the staircase and continued to climb. I licked salt from my lips as we reached the lantern room at the very top and cringed at the thought of how high up we were. I knew if I hesitated now then I might flee the lighthouse and never look back, so I forced myself forward and stepped over the threshold.

The huge windows up here were stormproof, and most of them were intact, apart from one that was partly smashed right at the top. There were bits of broken glass and dead gannets scattered everywhere. Several live birds flew around the tall room too. The revolving light made their shadows into gigantic, winged monsters for a moment before shrinking them back down to small specks.

I thought at first that we were alone in the lantern room, but then I spotted a small figure standing at one of the windows – a child dressed in rags. Even facing away from me, I saw that he was horribly thin. And there were dreadful wounds on his arms and legs, raw and red and messy. It took me a moment to realize what they were, but then I remembered my own injured leg and shivered. Those were eel bites.

I felt a great, powerful rush of sympathy that took the edge off my fear as I walked over and stopped behind him. Now that I was closer, I could hear that Conall was muttering a name under his breath. "Charlie! Charlie! *Charlie!*"

I took a deep breath and crouched down to his level.

"Hello, Conall," I said quietly. "I'm Jess. I'm so sorry for what happened to you."

He slowly turned to face me, and it took all

my willpower not to scream. His face was a mess. A great chunk of flesh had been bitten off by the eel, and I could see right through to his cheekbone beneath.

"Where's Charlie?" he asked. Part of his lower lip had been bitten off, which made him sound as if he was slobbering when he spoke.

"He's gone," I said. "He had to go home."

"He's afraid of me," Conall said in that wet, slobbering voice. "Everyone is, even Papa. Just because I killed that man."

"What happened in the workhouse wasn't your fault," I began. "It was—"

"No, not him," Conall said dully. "The other one. The keeper."

I paused. "Keeper?"

"Papa didn't like it when I killed the keeper." He looked at me with raw pleading in his eyes. "I didn't want to do it either, not really. The lighthouse got me all mixed up and made me think it was a good idea. Will you tell Charlie I'm sorry, and that I won't ever do it again? Perhaps then he'll come back."

I glanced at Will but he looked as confused as I felt.

"Are you talking about Niall Abernathy?" I asked.

"Yes, that's him. He was… Oh, if I try to tell you, I'll get it wrong – I *always* get it wrong – and then you'll be cross with me too. But it really wasn't my fault – it w*asn't*. Look."

Before I could say anything, he reached out and gripped my hand. His palm felt damp, and I barely had time to realize that one of his fingers had been chewed away entirely. But then Conall, the lighthouse and the storm vanished, and I was suddenly in the kitchen of the keeper's cottage on another day and time altogether.

Sun streamed through the windows, and a bearded man in a keeper's uniform sat across from me.

"Do you understand what I'm saying, Conall?" he said. "There's another keeper being stationed here, and we've got to keep you hidden from him. There's no other way. It won't be pleasant, and I'm truly sorry for that, but if he knew about you then he'd turn us into the police, and both our necks would be on the line. It won't be forever. Just until I finish my service at the lighthouse. When it's time to leave Bird Rock, everything will have died down back home – no one will be looking for us any more. I'll smuggle you out, and we'll make a new life for ourselves somewhere."

He was looking right at me, and I realized that I wasn't myself at all. My feet barely touched the kitchen floor, and I could feel emotions that weren't mine.

"All right, Papa."

The words came from my throat, but it wasn't my voice. I was inside Conall's body, seeing everything from his eyes. Which meant that the man in front of me must be his father, Finn Lewis – or Finn Jackson. He went on to say that there was a secret room inside the lighthouse, and Conall would have to stay there when the other keeper arrived. He'd bring food and supplies as often as he could, but they had to be careful because the only entrance was in the kitchen, and they couldn't risk the other keeper seeing.

Finn repeated that Conall must never, ever come out of the room. The only exception was if it flooded, which it might do if there was a storm. Conall knew the rules, he *knew* them, and he stuck to them for a while – as long as he could – but as the days and weeks passed by, it got harder and harder. It was cold and dark and lonely in the basement. It made his skull hurt, and I could feel that same ache inside my own head as Conall remembered it.

Being all alone in the dark made dark thoughts come to him too, the darkest thoughts he'd ever known, and having them in my own mind now made me feel dirty and damaged, and like I'd never be truly myself again. He couldn't stop thinking about how everything had been fine before the other keeper had arrived and ruined it all. So one night he sneaked out. The carving knives had been left out for cleaning, and Conall looked at them, and a plan formed in his mind.

The clock on the wall said it was three in the morning. He knew his papa had the late shift that night, which meant the other keeper would be asleep in his bed. Conall took the largest knife from the worktop, then made his way up the spiral staircase. He wasn't sure where the other man might be but eventually he found it was the same room he'd been using himself until he'd had to go to the basement – the beautiful one right near the top of the tower, so ornate and comfortable. When he crept in, the moon shone brightly through the window, clearly illuminating the Strangers' Room as it had been in its heyday, with fine oak furniture, a library of leather-bound books and soft Turkish rugs upon the mosaicked floor. The moon also illuminated the man in the bed.

It was the first time Conall had ever seen him, and he felt another great surge of anger towards him for ruining everything. His rage filled my own body, and the sheer force of it made me shudder as I realized that Conall truly hated this man. The lighthouse seemed to hold its breath around him, and Conall could sense how much the old stones *wanted* him to do it. How pleased they would be if he went ahead.

So he lifted the knife and plunged it straight into the man's throat. He fully expected him to die instantly and quietly, and I felt the shock ripple through Conall when blood sprayed into his face and the keeper lunged up with a wet, gurgling, inhuman groan. Conall struggled to keep a tight grip on the slippery knife as he raced into the corner, and watched in terror as the keeper flailed round the room, blood pouring from his throat to splatter over the rugs, the panelled walls, the marble fireplace, the bedding. It seemed to go everywhere. Conall had had no idea that a man contained so much blood.

When the man finally crashed to the floor, Conall longed to turn and run from the room as fast as possible, but he could feel a dark, ancient hunger emanating from the lighthouse's stones – and now I sensed it too. It was impossible to know if it was real, or Conall's imagination, but it really felt as if the lighthouse was willing him to finish the job.

Conall didn't want to make the lighthouse angry, so he advanced with the knife and stabbed the keeper a few more times, desperately trying to end it. Yet even then the man wasn't dead. Conall was shocked and confused and afraid. The only other person he'd killed had been that warden back at the workhouse – an accident, yet he had died the second his head struck the floor. It had all been over so quickly. Almost peacefully. This wasn't like that at all. Conall even began to wonder whether the keeper was a demon who couldn't be killed.

Not knowing what else to do, he sat back and watched. He could hear the keeper breathing – a horrible, rasping, rattling noise that made it sound as if each breath was destined to be his last, yet still he lingered on and on until, finally, Conall's father Finn came to rouse his partner for the morning shift.

Conall thought his papa would be pleased by what he'd done. He had solved their problem. Now the two of them could be together in the lighthouse once again. Only Finn wasn't pleased. Conall could tell just by looking at his face.

The dying keeper gave a slightly louder gurgle when he saw Conall's father, but that was the only sound he could make – his throat was too slashed to speak. Finn's hand trembled slightly as he asked Conall to hand him the knife. When it was clasped in his hand, he plunged it deep into the other keeper's chest, and at last he stopped gurgling and lay still.

Then Conall's father led him downstairs, but he didn't speak the whole time. Conall knew something was wrong when his father asked him to climb down the stairs into the secret room.

"But I don't need to live there any more, Papa," he pointed out.

"Best go and fetch up your blankets then," Finn said in a gruff tone.

Conall thought that made sense, so he went down the ladder but he'd barely descended before his father slammed the trapdoor closed on top of him, pinching his fingers in the gap and knocking him on the head so that he fell the remaining distance to the floor with a crash. He cried out but even then he still believed it was an accident – that his father would come down after him, exclaiming and apologizing. Only he didn't. Instead, he slid something heavy over the hatch so that Conall couldn't push it open again. Later, he heard him fastening locks to the trapdoor too. I felt the wave of claustrophobia hit Conall so forcefully that he thought he might drown in it.

Conall shouted up to him the entire time, demanding to know what was happening, but his father never spoke a word. Not until right at the end when he came to tell Conall he was leaving.

"You mean a boat's coming for us?" Conall asked hopefully.

"Not us," his father replied in his gruff tone. "Just me. I signalled a merchant vessel to take me off. Had to pay 'em a lot of money to keep it a secret, but it'll be worth it to start a new life elsewhere."

"But Papa—"

"There's something rotten in you, Conall.

There must be. After what you did to Niall…
As God is my witness, I hope I never live to see such
violence again."

"But Papa, I did it for *us*!" Conall wailed.
"And because the lighthouse wanted me to."

But it was no use. Finn was already gone.

Conall was convinced he would return at first,
but as time wore on he realized his father really
wasn't coming back, and he became scared. I could
feel his fear soaking through every single cell of
my body, and it was a raw terror unlike anything
I'd ever known before. A feeling so intense it was
surely enough to break down his mind entirely.
He screamed for help, he clawed at the trapdoor
until his nails were bloody.

There was no food or water in the room.
He'd thought being hungry was bad, but thirst was
the worst thing of all. It burned him like fire from
the outside in, until even his throat and tongue and
lips felt scorched with it. I felt it all just as he did,
and panic rose up inside me. This was what it must
feel like to die, and dying was icy, sharp and so very
lonely.

When the room became partially flooded, he still

couldn't drink anything because it was seawater. Seawater that brought the eel. Finally he sat down and used the last of the candle's light to write a letter to his mother. Then he turned his attention to the eel. I felt his joy at seeing another living thing, his hopes of making friends with it, of not being alone in the dark any more. When it bit him the first time, Conall tried to escape by climbing up on the table. But he couldn't stay awake there forever, and once he fell asleep he inevitably slumped and fell into the water. By then, he was too weak to get back up again. And so the eel could take as many bites out of him as it liked.

It was impossible to tell for sure whether it was dehydration, the eel or drowning that finally did it, but Conall was dead just a couple of days after his father left. And the great, awful rage he still felt over what had happened was like a ball of fire inside his chest, one that could never be extinguished.

Except ... when he'd seen Charlie, he'd thought that here at last might be a companion for him. A friend to take the edge off his loneliness. But Conall had never been very skilled at making friends, and he had failed here too, frightening

Charlie away in spite of his efforts – at least at first – to be gentle and careful. He hadn't even allowed Charlie to see his face in case he scared him, but it had all been for nothing. Whatever he did, it was never enough…

The dark dreadfulness of the shared vision ended abruptly and I found myself back in the lantern room with Will, and Conall, and the dozens of dead birds.

Chapter Twenty-four

"Will you bring Charlie back now?" Conall asked, watching me carefully. "You do understand, don't you? You know why I had to do those things, and that it wasn't my fault? The lighthouse *wanted* me to kill him. It wanted me to be bad."

"Of course," I said, standing up and stepping over to Will. "Of course I understand. But Charlie is … he can't come back here. He needs to go home. There were children in the fog," I said, my mind working quickly. "I saw them. Can't you make friends with one of them?"

A flicker of movement caught my eye, and I realized that the white hands were back again. I could see them pressed up against one of the parabolic mirrors – several pairs squeezed together –

as pale and beseeching as ever.

"They didn't want to be friends with me either," Conall said, his wet voice full of bitterness. "That's why they're forgotten people."

"How did they come to be forgotten, Conall?" I asked.

I recalled what he had written in his letters, his dread of being left alone and forgotten in the basement.

He gave a slight shrug, suddenly looking sullen. "I push them into the mirror," he said. "The one in the Strangers' Room."

"Is that what happened to my sister?" I asked.

Conall fixed me with a dark look. "She was just like the others," he said. "Searching all over for me, looking for me as if she wanted to be my friend, but when I came out of hiding and showed myself to her, she wasn't pleased to find me. Just afraid like all the others. So I pushed her into the mirror and then the world forgets her, just like it forgot me. And it serves her right."

"How do you get those people back out?" I asked.

"You don't!" he snapped. "If they don't want to be my friend, then they stay there forever."

"And what about *my* sister?" Will asked. "Kenzie. She saw you here last year. Why did you kill her rather than push her into the mirror? Was it because I said the words about how I knew you were there?"

"No one can know I'm here!" Conall looked suddenly wild-eyed. "No one! Papa told me I mustn't be found out, or bad things would happen."

"We wouldn't have hurt you," Will said, his voice catching in his throat. "There was no need for you to kill Kenzie."

"I was *trying* to drag her to the mirror," Conall replied. "But she yanked herself away and fell through the window. It wasn't my fault – it was an accident."

The mirror was white with hands now, just as the cliffs of Bird Rock turned white with gannets. One of the hands was pressing so hard against the surface that it looked as if it was about to come straight through to the other side again.

"You're still to blame," I said. "Rosie and Kenzie would both be here if it wasn't for you."

Conall's eyes narrowed, and black wells of hatred suddenly burned in his gaze. "They never should have been here in the first place!" he growled. "None of you should be here. It's *my* lighthouse.

So if you're not going to bring Charlie back then get out! Get OUT! *GET OUT!*"

His lips drew back in a snarl, and his eyes darkened as he glared at us. Then to our dismay, the tower began to shake. Perhaps it was the storm, or the power of Conall's sudden rage, but either way we could feel the floor trembling beneath our feet and the broken glass in the window rattling free of the panes. The second parabolic mirror was full of hands now too, some of which were beating on the glass. I realized we had made a mistake in coming up here. A second later, the door leading to the staircase slammed closed, and when I hurried over to open it, it was stuck fast.

"I'll be your friend," Will suddenly said, raising his voice over the fierce new howl of the wind. "If that's what you want."

I spun round. What was he doing?

Conall stared at him with open suspicion. "Why?" He spat the word out like a stone.

"Because I think that the way you are is not entirely your fault. And I think you've been alone for longer than any person should have to be. And I don't want you to hurt anyone else, even if it's by accident."

"Will you stay for*ever*?" Conall asked.

"Yes."

"Prove it!"

"How?" Will asked.

He wants me to do something bad...

Charlie's words echoed inside my head, and I already knew what Conall was going to say.

"You can't stay with me – you can't really be friends with me – if you're alive." He pointed to the balcony outside. "So jump, and then I'll know you're telling the truth."

I hurried back over to grab Will's sleeve. "*No!*"

"And if I do that then Jess can leave?" Will asked, ignoring me and looking at Conall.

"Yes."

"And you promise you won't ever hurt anyone again?"

"I promise," Conall said, eyes gleaming as he reached for Will's hand and began tugging him over to the door leading outside.

I tried to yank him back, but Will was much stronger than me.

"It's all right, Jess," he said. "This is what I came

320

to the island to do."

It wasn't what *I* had come here for, though. I was here to save my sister, not lose a friend. So I did the only thing I could think of – I rugby-tackled him to the ground. He was much bigger than me but I had the element of surprise, and he crashed to the floor. He grunted and pushed me off, while Conall looked on, scowling.

"Jess, what the hell?" Will dragged himself back to his feet. "You have to let me do this. Otherwise people will keep on dying and vanishing on Bird Rock."

I scrambled up just as a flash of lightning lit the sky. To my horror, I thought I saw the silhouette of an old woman crouched on the rails of the balcony outside, leering at me. The next second, she was gone, as if she'd never been there at all.

I took a deep breath. "I am *not* going to— Hey!"

I broke off as Will lunged for the door. I grabbed hold of his arm but he twisted out of my grasp and slipped through before slamming the door behind him and leaning against it to stop me following. Conall appeared beside him, brushed his hand over the door, and a lock thudded into place so that I still couldn't open it, even once Will stepped back.

I'm sorry, he mouthed, before turning away.

Everything was moving too fast, and my head spun, trying to work out what to do. I couldn't let this happen – I *couldn't*. The part of the window that was broken was too high for me to reach, so I gazed around the room, looking for something I could use as a weapon to smash the lower part of the glass. Then my eye fell on the mirror. I saw the hands again, only this time they were different. One of them was holding something. I saw a flash of pink and realized it was a piece of crystal – of rose quartz – in the shape of an angel. *Rosie's* angel.

I raced to the mirror. The hand with the angel had been swallowed up by the others that were now reaching through, but finally I found it again. I didn't hesitate. I wrapped my fingers tightly around the hand. The skin was smooth and icy cold to the touch – like taking the hand of a statue. A jolt ran through me, and my whole body shuddered. But then the hand became firmer and warmer beneath my grasp, began to feel like skin and muscle rather than stone. I heaved with all my might and slowly, surely, an arm followed the hand, then a shoulder, and then Rosie's head was there, and she was crying with relief as she came out of the mirror and fell into my arms. She smelled of birds and fog and was shivering from head to foot, but she was here and she was alive.

"Are you OK?" I asked.

She nodded. "I am now."

I allowed myself one blissful moment of holding her close, but that was all we had time for.

When I looked back at the balcony, I saw that Will was standing right at the edge, Conall by his side. I couldn't hear what was being said, if anything, but I guessed it was nothing good. Will's shoulders suddenly straightened and he reached out to grip the edge of the rails.

"The others!" I gasped. "If we get them out too, will they help us stop Conall?"

I didn't want to unleash more potentially angry spirits if they weren't going to help, but Rosie nodded and said, "His anger is what's been keeping them here."

We each reached for a hand and tugged. Two more lost people stepped through the mirror. It seemed to be easier for them now that Rosie had paved a way by doing it once. Perhaps it was simpler too because they didn't have solid bodies like hers. Even if they'd been alive when they'd first vanished, they were now long-since dead, their bodies were thin and insubstantial, and their hands felt like they were barely there. First the keeper and then the woman I'd seen in the fog both emerged from the mirror. I guessed it was the first time they hadn't been lost in fog or mirror worlds since their disappearance, and they wasted no time. Together, they flew through the windows of the lantern room and descended on Conall just as Will climbed up on to the rails.

Conall struggled and fought in their grip, but they were two adults against one child, and together they dragged him back through the glass, into the lantern room, and thrust him against the dozens of eager hands still reaching out from the mirror.

"No!" he hissed, fury contorting his ravaged features. "You can't take me from the lighthouse! It's mine! It's—!"

But that was as far as he got before the hands closed over his mouth and face and limbs. His whole body vanished into the mirror, and the keeper and the woman went after him. And then the glass was empty. No ghosts, no hands, just ordinary glass reflecting the room back at us. And in that reflection I saw Will perched on the railing. He was facing us and had clearly seen what had happened. There was relief and delight on his face, and he was already lifting his leg to climb back to safety.

But then a bolt of lightning forked through the sky and struck the tower, smashing up part of the balcony. The impact made the entire lighthouse shudder alarmingly, smashing the broken window and shaking the door free of its hinges. The rails there were very old and couldn't take the impact. The section Will clung to came free with a hideous squealing of metal.

It all happened in a flash.

One moment Will was there.

The next ... he wasn't.

Chapter Twenty-five

"WILL!" My shout was so loud that it felt like something in my throat actually tore.

He was gone. As if satisfied that it had done its worst, the storm suddenly calmed down too. The wind dropped and the rain slowed to a steady patter rather than driving needles.

"Oh God." I turned to Rosie. "Stay here, OK?"

She nodded, her eyes huge. The thought of stepping out on to that balcony appalled me, especially as I didn't know how structurally sound the rest of it might be, but if there was any chance of helping Will – if he wasn't already lying dead at the base of the tower – then I had to do it.

I climbed out through the broken window. The gap was only just about big enough, and

I broke off more bits of glass as I pushed through. The balcony was slick with rainwater, and pieces of window crunched underfoot. My head spun at the sight of Bird Rock sprawled below us, especially as there were no railings between me and the unthinkable drop. I felt truly, utterly sick as I crept to the edge, fully expecting to see Will's broken body lying at the base of the tower, just as Kenzie's had been a year earlier.

But when I reached the edge, I saw him dangling just below me. Impossibly, incredibly, his jacket had become caught on one of the protruding nails attached to the bracket for the railings, allowing him time to find fingerholds on the exposed bricks. He was clinging to these like a limpet, but I could see he wouldn't be able to stay there for long. Already, his fingertips were bleeding and turning white with the strain.

"Will," I whispered, not daring to speak his name loudly in case it startled him and caused him to fall.

He looked up, his eyes widening when he saw me, and he swore under his breath. "Get away from the edge!" he snapped. "This whole thing could go at any moment."

I dropped to my stomach and reached over to grab hold of his arm.

"If we're going to be friends," I said, "you've got to stop telling me what to do."

"What's the point of trying to tell you what to do?" he groaned. "You never listen."

I looked for something to hook my foot into so that I could take Will's weight without being dragged over the edge myself, but there was nothing on the balcony to grab hold of.

"You've got to leave," he begged. "Please."

The great drop spun dizzyingly below, and I could hardly breathe through my proximity to the edge. But if Will was stuck then I was too.

"I'm not leaving," I said. "No way. Not without you."

I was just wondering whether I could yell back at Rosie to go and look for some rope or something when she suddenly appeared behind me and gripped my ankle.

"It's OK!" she called. "I've got my legs hooked through the railings. You can pull him up."

I felt a bit annoyed that Rosie had ignored my instruction to stay put – which I suppose was kind of ironic, given the circumstances – but the priority was getting us all off this lighthouse, so I grabbed hold of Will's arm with both hands and pulled.

It turns out that hauling a person's weight up like that is ridiculously hard, and I could feel my arms and shoulders screaming with the effort, the muscles stretching and tearing as I dragged him inch by torturous inch. Will did his best to help, gripping the edge as soon as he could and taking some of the weight, but still the cut glass beneath me dug deeper and deeper into my skin. For a moment, I thought I saw the hunched, angry shape of the bean nighe on the ground far below, then she melted away into the darkness and Will was sprawled on the balcony beside me.

Rosie was on her feet at once, helping us both scrabble back to the relative safety of the lantern room. The rain softened to a gentle pattering, before finally ceasing altogether. When I looked out, I saw that the sky was starting to lighten, already tinged with pink. Dawn had arrived. We had survived the night.

"Jess Oliver," Will finally said. "You are the most infuriating girl I ever met."

"Thanks," I replied. "And you're welcome."

He sighed. "It wasn't meant as a compliment, but … thank you. I can't believe you did that." His eyes went to my sister. "Hello, Rosie. I hope you're all right?"

"Hi, Will. And yes, I think I'll be fine."

"We should go," I said. "I don't know about you two, but I've had enough of this lighthouse."

"Agreed," Will said. "Let's get out of here."

As we made our way back down the spiral staircase, the lighthouse felt different – calmer, more peaceful. There were no weird taps or clicks behind the walls, no ominous groaning from the pipes, no nails scratching over glass. There was just the distant roar of the sea and the call of the birds outside. Yet as we walked I began to feel odd. I was still drenched to the skin and shivering slightly, but I was suddenly hot at the same time, and it became more difficult to catch my breath. I figured perhaps it was just the shock finally kicking in. We reached the ground floor and walked out into the weak morning sunshine.

"I'm never going into a lighthouse again as long as I live!" Rosie exclaimed. She turned towards me.

"God, I've got so much to tell you, Jess, about being lost in the fog and trapped behind the mirror and— Hey, are you OK? You look weird."

"I don't know," I replied, and my voice sounded slurred. "I just feel really…"

The words seemed to float away from me, and a cloud of confusion filled my brain as the ground wobbled beneath my feet. Will's steadying hands were on me at once, but the strength drained out of my legs and I pulled him down with me as I crumpled to the floor.

That's when I realized that the wetness around my ribs wasn't just from the rain. It was warm and sticky, and there was a large shard of glass sticking out of my T-shirt. As soon as I saw it, I dimly registered the pain for the first time too, a dull throbbing that started in my side and then ran all the way up my spine to my brain.

"It's all right," Will said. "It's going to be all right."

He sounded really far away, and when I looked up, I saw my own panic reflected in his face.

"Jess?" His hands tightened round my arms. "Don't close your eyes. Listen. You've got to…"

But I didn't hear any more of what he said

because a heavy wave swept in, wrapping me up in it like a dark blanket.

When I woke up a short while later, we were back at the guga hunters' camp. Cailean had carefully wrapped bandages around my wound, although the glass was still lodged there. He said it would be dangerous to remove it on Bird Rock, and that it would have to wait until we were on the mainland.

The rescue boat would be here in an hour or so, and it couldn't come soon enough for me. I wanted to get off Bird Rock and never look back. It didn't help that Dad and Kate were furious with us for going back to the lighthouse. It was almost a good thing I'd hurt myself, because at least it meant their anger was tempered with worry.

As for Rosie, she just seemed to slip straight back in with everyone as if she'd never been gone. Everybody knew who she was, and no one seemed to realize there had been a time when she was forgotten at all. Charlie seemed oddly upset for some reason, and rushed over to me, mumbling something incoherent that I couldn't make sense of.

In the end, he burst into tears and Kate took him away to a quiet corner.

While the others all helped pack up the camp around us, Rosie whispered to me about how she'd gone up to the Strangers' Room that night only to find herself face to face with Conall. When she reacted to him with fear, he'd pushed her through to the other side of the mirror, where she became lost in the fog.

"There were other people there too. They never spoke to me, and I never spoke to them. It's hard to remember them now. I didn't feel like myself in the fog – I didn't feel like a person at all. I never thought to ask any of the others about what was happening. It was as if it was just too much effort to speak. But I saw that they were always trying to get back into the lighthouse and reach the boy, Conall, and it felt like something I should do too. I knew that he was responsible, somehow, for what had happened to us. Sometimes we'd make it as close as a window, or one of the mirrors inside, but we could never break through, at least not for long."

"The hands," I said. "That's what they were the whole time." I glanced at my sister. "I think some of the keepers remembered the people who were forgotten too, and that's why they were taken off to asylums. Other keepers just seemed to have a nagging doubt that something was wrong or missing, but they didn't know what. Anyway, I'm glad it's over. I love you."

I gripped Rosie's hand. God, I'd missed her. "I'm so glad you're all right."

"Me too." She squeezed my fingers tight. "And thanks, Jess, for coming after me."

"I'll always come after you. Anywhere you go, I go too."

After the events of the day before, everyone was wary of the gannets, but none of the birds came anywhere near us as the hunters packed up their camp. Will and I speculated that perhaps they were no longer being influenced by the lighthouse now that Conall's angry presence had gone.

A short while later, the boat arrived, everything was packed and ready, and we all went aboard. I was relieved to find that because this was an emergency rescue boat it had a warm, comfortable inside bit, and I was stationed there as the only person with a piece of glass sticking out of them. There was a window, though, and I watched as we sailed away from Bird Rock, the lighthouse growing smaller and smaller behind us. It was a relief when it finally vanished over the horizon. I felt like I could breathe easily again for the first time in a long while.

Dad stuck close by me for most of the trip and so did Rosie, but at one point I persuaded them to go out on deck for some air, and Will came in to chat to me. After a while, I said something about how well Rosie had slipped back into the group.

"What do you mean?" Will asked, looking puzzled.

"Well, it was like she was there all along," I said. "Like she was never forgotten."

Will stared at me, and it soon became clear that he had absolutely no idea what I was talking about.

"You really don't remember?" I asked. "You don't remember that Rosie disappeared, and everyone forgot her?"

Will frowned. "No, I don't. Are you ... are you joking?"

I shuddered. "I don't think it's possible to joke

about Bird Rock. Look, forget it. It doesn't matter any more. We got away, didn't we?"

"Yeah," Will replied, but he looked distracted, and I could tell he wasn't paying attention to me properly.

"Hey," I finally said, waving my hand in front of his face. "Earth to Will! Are you listening?"

He looked at me. "Sorry. I zoned out for a moment."

"Don't worry. It's been a lot. But I thought maybe, after everything we've been through, we could go and get a milkshake or something on the mainland? Once I'm better. If you want to, I mean."

"Sounds good," Will replied.

"Are you sure you're OK?" I asked. "It seems like there's something on your mind."

"I'm just… I've been thinking about what you said before. About Rosie. If that's true, then it means we can't trust our memories about what happened on the island." His eyes met mine. "We can't be sure that we didn't leave someone else behind."

I paused. I hadn't thought of that, and it was unsettling. "I don't think we did," I finally said.

"No," Will said firmly. "I'm sure you're right."

336

He glanced at the horizon. "Soon we'll be on the mainland and we can put all this behind us and go for those milkshakes. It looks like we're almost there. I'm just going to head on deck and see if they need a hand."

The rest of the voyage passed uneventfully. I was too tired to talk to anyone and simply enjoyed being wrapped up in my blanket, finally able to relax in the knowledge that we'd escaped. We had all managed to get off Bird Rock in one piece. We had fought, and we had won. As the boat docked on the mainland, I felt more and more free. Relieved that I would never have to set foot on Bird Rock again.

Except … that's not what actually happened.

Postscript

The voyage as I've described it is honestly how I remember it happening. However, I know it wasn't quite like that because of the letter I later found in my pocket, hurriedly written in my own handwriting. I'm adding it to the record now, and it reads as follows:

I don't know how much time I have to set this down, so I've got to be quick. After Will left, Charlie came in to see me, and I had a disturbing conversation with him — one I'm afraid I will eventually forget. So here it is for future me, exactly as it happened.

"Did you see him?" Charlie asked. "Was he there at the lighthouse?"

I assumed he meant Conall and said, "Yes, but

don't worry, he's gone. He won't be able to hurt anyone again."

Charlie shook his head vigorously. "Not him," he said. "I meant Rory."

I frowned. "Who's Rory?"

Charlie's face fell. "My brother. We talked about him back at the hunters' camp, remember? You said you'd look for him inside the lighthouse, that you'd bring him home."

I stared at him, a growing feeling of horror creeping over my body. "I don't remember any Rory."

Charlie started to cry. "But you promised!" he said. "And you have to remember him. You talked to him and played board games with us, and he showed you his pet snails and gave you a welcome drawing when you first arrived at the lighthouse."

I shook my head. "That was you."

Charlie looked morose. "I hate drawing. And snails."

My head started to throb. "But do you mean ... are you saying that he was there with us? On Bird Rock the whole time?"

"Right until Mummy and me ran away from the

lighthouse and came to the guga hunters' camp,"
Charlie said. "I told you what had happened.
You didn't remember him then either, but you
believed me and said you'd try to get him back."

I remembered taking Charlie's hand at the camp
and promising him something, but when I wracked
my brain I just couldn't recall exactly what I had
promised or what we'd talked about.

When I thought back over our time at the
lighthouse, I remembered only one boy, but he
seemed an odd mixture of things, as if he had a
split personality. Not only that, but Dad and Kate
were always saying contradictory things about
him. Could that be because there had been two
boys all along? It was just that my brain had
merged them into one when I'd forgotten Rory.

Suddenly I thought of that board game Rosie and
I had played with Charlie during the storm.

"Please?" he'd said, over and over again. "We
need four people to play."

It was a four-person game, yet somehow we'd
played the game with only three of us. How had
we done that? Or could it be that there had been
four of us back then? I just couldn't remember.

"I'm so sorry, Charlie," I whispered. "I forgot that conversation. I don't remember Rory, but I do believe you."

His eyes filled with tears as he stared at me, and I felt like the absolute worst person in the world. One of those hands reaching through the glass had belonged to my half-brother, but I had forgotten him, and now he was still there, trapped inside the fog. And it was my fault.

I thought about going to the captain of the boat, seeing if I could persuade him to turn the vessel round right now and take us back to Bird Rock, but even as the thought occurred to me, I started to feel a weird tingly ache at the front of my head, one that seemed to burrow deep into my brain and make queasiness churn in my stomach. I was going to forget Rory again — forget our entire conversation. So I've set it all down here for my future self to find.

There were five of us in that lighthouse, not four.

We left someone behind.

And so one day, whatever it takes, we've got to get back to Bird Rock.

Acknowledgements

Many thanks to the following people:

My agent, Thérèse Coen, and the Hardman and Swainson Literary Agency.

Katie Jennings, Ella Whiddett, Mattie Whitehead and Lauren Ace for editorial input. Jane Tait for copyediting and Susila Baybars for proofreading. Pip Johnson for the amazing cover. Dannie Price and Summer Lanchester for marketing and publicity. Demet Hoffmeyer for production, George Hanratty for sales, and Nicola O'Connell for managing rights. And to everyone else at Stripes for all their hard work on this book.

Finally, thank you to my family, for their continuous support.

Alex Bell is the best-selling author of *Frozen Charlotte*, *Charlotte Says* and *The Haunting* in Stripes' YA horror series, RED EYE. Alex lives in Hampshire and also writes middle-grade fantasy books, including *The Polar Bear Explorers' Club*.

www.alex-bell.co.uk
@Alex_Bell86

We're
waiting
for you to
come and play

FROZEN CHARLOTTE

ALEX BELL

Dunvegan School for Girls has been
closed for many years. Converted into a
family home, the teachers and students are
long gone. But they left something behind…

Sophie arrives at the old schoolhouse to spend
the summer with her cousins. Brooding Cameron
with his scarred hand, strange Lilias with her
fear of bones and Piper, who seems just a
bit too good to be true. And then
there's her other cousin.

The girl with a room full of antique dolls.
The girl that shouldn't be there.
The girl that died.

Turn the page for an extract from

FROZEN CHARLOTTE

ALEX BELL

ISBN: 978-1-84715-453-8

RED EYE

Isle of Skye – 1910

The girls were playing with the Frozen Charlotte dolls again.

The schoolmistress had given them some scraps of fabric and ribbon from the sewing room to take out to the garden. They were to practise their embroidery skills by making little dresses and bonnets for the naked porcelain dolls. "They'll catch their death of cold otherwise," the teacher had said.

But there was one girl who wasn't playing with the others. The schoolmistress sighed when she saw her, sat alone, fiddling with her blindfold. The girl complained it was uncomfortable but the doctor had said it was necessary to keep her wound clean. And, besides, the sight of her ruined eyes frightened the other girls.

The schoolmistress got up and went over to her,

just as she succeeded in untying the knot.

"Now, Martha," she said, deftly tying it back up again. "Remember what the doctor said."

The girl hung her head and said nothing. She hadn't spoken much since the accident. Not since the doctor had come and Martha had made those ridiculous accusations.

"Why don't you go and join the girls in their game?" the schoolmistress said.

The blind girl shook her head and spoke so quietly that the teacher had to strain to hear. "It's a bad game."

"Nonsense. Come along now and play with the others. I'm sure they can help you if you ask."

She took Martha's hand and tugged her, stumbling along, to where the girls were playing in the sunshine. But when she got there she found that they weren't making dresses for the dolls after all. They were making shrouds. And they'd covered the dolls up with them as if they were corpses. Some of the girls were even making little crosses out of twigs.

"What are you doing?" the schoolmistress said.

The girls looked up at her. "We're holding a funeral for the Frozen Charlottes, Miss Grayson."

"Well, stop it at once," the teacher replied. "I never heard of anything so ghoulish."

"But, miss," one of the girls said, "they like being dead. They told us."

SLEEPLESS
LOU MORGAN

ISBN: 978-1-84715-455-2

FROZEN
CHARLOTTE
ALEX BELL

ISBN: 978-1-84715-453-8

BAD
BONES
GRAHAM MARKS

ISBN: 978-1-84715-454-5

FLESH and
BLOOD
SIMON CHESHIRE

ISBN: 978-1-84715-456-9

THE
HAUNTING
ALEX BELL

ISBN: 978-1-84715-458-3

FIR
SHARON GOSLING

ISBN: 978-1-84715-823-9

CHARLOTTE
SAYS
ALEX BELL

ISBN: 978-1-84715-840-6

SAVAGE
ISLAND
BRYONY PEARCE

ISBN: 978-1-84715-827-7

WHITEOUT
GABRIEL DYLAN

ISBN: 978-1-78895-072-5

CRUEL
CASTLE
BRYONY PEARCE

ISBN: 978-1-78895-321-4

REDEYE

Do you dare?